GIRL LOST

A DETECTIVE KAITLYN CARR MYSTERY

KATE GABLE

D1103717

BYRD BOOKS LLC

COPYRIGHT

Visit my website at www.kategable.com

WANT TO BE THE FIRST TO KNOW ABOUT MY UPCOMING SALES, NEW RELEASES AND EXCLUSIVE GIVEAWAYS?

Sign up for my newsletter:
https://www.subscribepage.com/kategableviplist

Join my Facebook Group:
https://www.facebook.com/
groups/833851020557518

Bonus Points: Follow me on BookBub and Goodreads!

https://www.goodreads.com/author/show/21534224.Kate_Gable

ABOUT KATE GABLE

Kate Gable loves a good mystery that is full of suspense. She grew up devouring psychological thrillers and crime novels as well as movies, tv shows and true crime.

Her favorite stories are the ones that are centered on families with lots of secrets and lies as well as many twists and turns. Her novels have elements of psychological suspense, thriller, mystery and romance.

Kate Gable lives in Southern California with her husband, son, a dog and a cat. She has spent more than twenty years in this area and finds inspiration from its cities, canyons, deserts, and small mountain towns.

Write her here:

Kate@kategable.com

Check out her books here:

www.kategable.com

Sign up for my newsletter:
https://www.subscribepage.com/kategableviplist

Join my Facebook Group:
https://www.facebook.com/
groups/833851020557518

Bonus Points: Follow me on BookBub and
Goodreads!

bookbub.com/authors/kate-gable

https://www.goodreads.com/author/show/
21534224.Kate_Gable

ABOUT GIRL LOST

Don't save me...

A newlywed with a secret pregnancy goes missing after a business trip. Her husband isn't very concerned.

Why didn't he want to report her missing? Where is she? Why was she keeping her pregnancy a secret? **Detective Kaitlyn Carr has to get to the truth.**

But back home in Big Bear Lake, her thirteen-year-old sister is still missing and now her friend has disappeared as well under very similar circumstances. The FBI is called in and the agent assigned to the case is none other than Luke Galvinson. But the last thing Kaitlyn needs is a man from her past.

Kaitlyn must not only split her time between these cases but also go further down the rabbit hole of the place she once called home.

Nothing is what it seems.

No one is who they are.

Everyone has a secret.

Can Kaitlyn uncover the truth in time to prevent another death?

Girl Lost is a suspenseful thriller perfect for fans of A. J. Rivers, Mary Stone, Willow Rose, James Patterson, Melinda Leigh, Kendra Elliot, Ella Gray, and Karin Slaughter. It has mystery, angst, a bit of romance and family drama.

1

I don't want to be here, but I don't have a choice. This guy's wife is missing and no one else is available to do the initial interview. I need to go back home and help find my sister, but instead I find myself sitting in traffic in West Hollywood.

I grew up in these parts. Well, not really grew up, but this is where I became an adult. I attended the University of Southern California. My boyfriend at the time lived in Park La Brea Apartments on the other side of The Grove, a big open-air shopping district right off of Fairfax. It's a beautiful place with a farmers market, shops, Barnes & Noble, and an old-style multiplex and fountains. It's small enough to be quaint, no matter how many tourists show up looking for celebrity sightings.

Park La Brea Apartments are the fancy towers looking over LA, the tallest structures in either direction. I don't live too far away from here, but for some reason when an overzealous driver in a new Mercedes cuts me off and steals my parking spot my mind wanders.

I remember all of the hours that I have spent at that Barnes & Noble and The Grove and all the fun that we had walking back over to his apartment. We were juniors and we weren't the type to go to parties or participate in Greek life.

We wore black and read books written by authors from other countries with long names.

We liked being outsiders.

The husband lives in a second-floor walk-up on Willoughby Avenue. He comes out of the apartment even before I knock. Inviting me inside, he swallows hard and nervously cracks his knuckles.

"Thank you for coming," he says a little bit too quickly.

I don't know what to make of him at first. He's wearing a slouchy hat and his jeans are a little too baggy. In general, he looks just like any other mildly-employed guy in his late twenties walking around LA.

"You said that you wanted to make a report about your wife being missing?" I ask, partly surprised by the fact that someone like him even has a wife.

"Yes."

"Your name is Robert Kaslar?" I ask, pulling a small notebook out of my crossbody bag.

A few minutes later, a deputy with the face of a high school student comes in and introduces himself again.

"Gary Lenore, we've met," I say, shaking his hand.

"Yes, of course," Lenore mumbles. "I was just downstairs checking the parking lot."

"I already told you that her car isn't there," Mr. Kaslar barks.

"Detective Carr, can I speak with you for a moment?" Lenore asks, nudging me to speak to him in private.

He pulls me aside out on the landing and shows me his notes. I glance down his uniform and look straight into the camera on his vest, recording everything it sees and hears.

"So, what's going on?" I ask.

"I don't know. His wife's friend called it in."

"Really?" I ask, surprised.

"Where is she?"

"She had to go. She had to pick up her kid from school. She said that they were on a business trip together and they came home late last night and they had... She was going to have an appointment today at the gynecologist to confirm whether or not she's pregnant."

"Oh, wow. Okay," I say, nodding and jotting down a few quick notes.

"Anyway, they were supposed to meet up for lunch and she never showed," Lenore continues.

"Well, that's not that unusual, right?" I ask.

"I guess it is, for this girl."

"How old is she?" I ask.

"Twenty-seven."

"So how long has she been missing?"

"It's unclear. According to the husband, he hasn't seen her since this morning and her friend hasn't had contact with her since last night."

"Okay."

It's hard to tell what this all means.

I come back into the apartment and take a more careful look around. The place is very clean. Actually, it seems a little bit too spotless for the type of guy that Mr. Kaslar appears to be.

It's a one-bedroom with charcoal walls and white curtains, delicate and embroidered with little flowers. They sway lightly in the breeze from the open window. The walls are covered in photographs, pictures of them on their various trips together. There are photos from Maui, Key West, Cancun.

"You two travel a lot?" I ask.

"Yeah. Whenever we can, whenever time allows."

"What is it that you do, Mr. Kaslar?"

"It's *Dr.* Kaslar, actually."

"Okay. Dr. Kaslar. What is it that you do?" I ask again, surprised by the formality.

He shifts his weight from one foot to another, crossing his arms and practically holding onto his elbows.

"I just got my PhD in engineering at USC," he says. "Electrical engineering."

"Oh, got it. Congratulations."

"Yeah, whatever," he says, distracted.

He takes a step closer to me and, for a second, I think he's going to touch me, but he doesn't.

"Sorry. I don't know why I said that thing about calling me doctor," he says. "You don't have to. Just call me Robert. I'm just really discombobulated about this whole thing."

"Of course, I can only imagine," I say, with as much sympathy as I can muster. "Your wife's name is Karen Moore Kaslar, right?"

He nods.

"What is it that she does for a living?"

"She's a writer. I mean, she wants to be a writer. I don't know," he mumbles.

"Does she work anywhere?" I ask, deciding to narrow my focus.

I realize, of course, that this is Los Angeles where 'what you do for a living' means different things to different people. Here, many people drive Uber or waitress in restaurants while trying to get a semblance of a career in the entertainment industry.

"Karen writes short stories. She's thinking about doing an MFA program. She's not really working anywhere."

"Okay. Got it. Yeah." I look at my notes. "Her friend, Elin? She said that they went on a business trip together?"

He shifts his weight again and puts his hoodie up over his head and then down. He has short dark hair that looks like it hasn't been washed in days.

"Can you just help me find her? I'm lost without her," he says, looking straight into my eyes. His gaze is disarming and full of intensity.

"Yes, of course. That is why I'm here, but I really need some details first. What can you tell me about her friend Elin? She mentioned that they went on a business trip?" I ask, steering the conversation back to what I need him to answer.

"Yes, they did, but that has nothing to do with this," he says, growing irate.

"Please, Robert, I need you to be patient. You never know what kind of details are going to be important."

"Elin is just this girl she met at Jamba Juice," he says with exasperation. "I think they do yoga together. I don't know. Anyway, she got her all into this MLM."

"MLM?" I ask.

"Multilevel marketing. They also call it network marketing, but it's basically a pyramid scheme."

I nod.

"She had to invest like four grand into this candle business and then she has to contact people on Facebook and all of her old friends and try to sell it to them. She's not a salesperson. Even if she were, this MLM thing makes no sense. You make more money getting people to become salespeople than actually selling products. The only people that make any money with it are the ones at the very top. Everyone else just ends up losing."

I can hear the anger in his voice, so I just let him talk.

"I tried to explain this to her," Robert continues. "I tried to show her all of these YouTube videos and all of these people talking about how much money they lost, but she just wouldn't listen."

The urgency in his voice is difficult to ignore. He's so angry and upset by this whole thing and he's not even trying to hide it.

"So, it's safe to say that you and Elin are not on the best terms?" I ask.

"No. Yeah, that's safe to say," he says.

"Is that what she was on the trip for?"

"She went on this trip for like three days, I think. Two days, maybe, to Phoenix. I have been working on this really big project that I just started and I've been staying at the office."

"Is that something that's common for you?"

"No. Well, I don't know. I always worked late. Doing a PhD isn't the easiest thing in the world, but I never had to stay overnight. With this new job, everything's different. They kind of took me on and there was so much work to do. So, since she was going to be away, I just decided to work and that's what I did."

"Okay. Got it."

Officer Lenore and I exchange a glance. It's hard for me to decide what I really think about Robert. He seems frantic and out of control, but that's not uncommon when a loved one is missing. Then there are certain things that feel a little bit off.

"Would you mind if I take a look around your apartment?" I ask.

"Sure. Yeah. Can I get you anything to drink?" he asks.

"No, I'm good." I walk around and Officer Lenore follows closely from behind.

"What are we looking for?" he whispers.

"I don't know. Just looking at things," I say in a hushed tone. "You see the bed? It's unmade. I don't know what that means. It may mean that he's not someone who makes his bed, or it may mean that today is unusual."

I pull the sheets and look underneath. There is nothing visible to the eye, nothing that catches my attention.

I look up at the windows, same perfect white trim all around, also open. I wouldn't say that's particularly unusual.

"Robert, can I ask you a question?" I yell for him to come over.

"Sure."

"The curtains, what happened to this one over here?"

Instead of the usual four panels, there are actually only three. The window looks like someone has tried to cover this up without much success.

"Oh, that? Nothing."

"Can you tell me what happened?"

"It was really stupid actually." Robert laughs.

He hesitates and swallows hard. When I try to focus my eyes on his, he avoids contact.

I wait for him to explain.

The moment of silence that forms seems to last forever, but I wait anyway. I want him to feel it. This is the type of moment when people crack, when people admit something that they shouldn't, at least, the things that they shouldn't say in their best interest.

"Nothing happened," he says.

Shifting his weight again, he pulls the hoodie over his head.

"It's just, it's stupid. I didn't buy enough panels. These were only available at Ikea. So, when we were decorating this house, I just bought two, but I needed to buy two more. I had to drive all the way back to Burbank to get them. I wasn't really happy about that. We had a fight, but she was insistent that the curtains out in the living room and the ones in this bedroom had to match. It was so stupid. Anyway, I went back out again, came back the third time, and I thought that we were all set."

"Why a third time?" I ask.

"Well, the first time was for the ones in the living room. The second time was for these, but this wasn't enough to block all the light and she didn't want to get darkening ones. She thought that we could just double up. Anyway, I went out to get them again and… The thing is that there was only one panel instead of two."

"What do you mean?" I ask.

He shakes his head. His face gets flushed and I can feel the tension as he's brought back to that moment.

"Somebody stole one! It's so dumb. I drove all the way back there and I was not going to do it again. Anyway, I don't want to make Karen sound like she's a nutcase because she's not. She's just really anal about certain things and she wanted me to go back, but I refused. I said I'd been there three times. We had a fight about it, and she refused to go on principle. What principle, I have no idea."

"Okay. So, what happened?"

"This. This is what happened."

"So, you just, what, like had a stalemate?"

"Yes, exactly. Neither of us would budge. So, we just have three. That's it. How is this important to you finding her?"

"At this point, I have no idea what is important."

"Listen, I really don't want to tell you how to do your job, but you really have to go find her," he says. "I mean, she's my wife. She can't just be gone."

I nod. I'm wondering for a second how this whole conversation got so off course in the wrong direction.

"So, let's just review," I say.

He walks out of the bedroom, but Lenore and I remain. I make one long scan around, king-size bed, plush. The bed is a metal platform bed painted white. One of those that look like the beds popular in the past.

There are two nightstands. One is completely covered in books about writing and short story collections. The other is perfectly neat with nothing but a small lamp on the side.

"Is that your side?" I ask.

"Yeah, she's not exactly a neat freak," Robert says with a smile.

"Got it."

I thought that he had walked away, but instead he's just hovering in the hallway.

The closet is rather small, and the doors have glass on the windows on the outside. I slide one open and look inside. It's stuffed with things. There's so much clothing from the top to the bottom that I can barely get the door closed again. For a second, I wonder if maybe her body is hidden somewhere in there, but I don't smell anything. I'm tempted to ask him for permission to go through it but if he says no, I'll need a warrant and I don't want our relationship to escalate to that level right now. I need him to cooperate.

Walking out of the bedroom and past the bathroom, I don't note anything out of the ordinary. It's a typical 1970s apartment with a small toilet and a minuscule sink. A bunch of lotion and makeup bottles crowd the back wall since the additional cabinet above the toilet is already completely full.

When I peek into the shower, I notice that the tub looks clean, but not so clean like someone had recently bleached it.

Back in the living room, I find Robert sitting on the overstuffed reclining couch facing the 60-inch television. Both of their desks are located in the dining room section.

His is pristine with just the laptop and a printer. Hers is covered with piles of papers, folders, notebooks, and library books. Somewhere underneath I see a laptop barely sticking out.

There are five black bookshelves that go all the way to the ceiling, each packed with titles. Some contain classics like *The Iliad* and others are in Greek and Latin. The ones near her desk contain collections of Faulkner, Hemingway, Austen, as well as Mansfield and Irving. Other popular ones like John Grisham, Jill James, and Stephenie Meyer appear as well.

"She has quite varied interests, I see," I say, pointing to the Twilight collection.

"Yeah. Actually, no, not really. Recently she started reading more popular stuff. I think she was getting very disappointed with the publishing prospects of short stories and she just wanted to make money. So, she started expanding her horizons of what's possible and what she can do."

"That's good," I say. "So why don't you tell me, again, everything that led up to you discovering that she was missing."

2
___

"**I**'m not sure what you want me to say," Robert says, walking over to the kitchen and starting to pour himself a cup of tea.

He grabs a tea bag out of the cabinet above the teapot and opens it in such a way that it rips the bag in half.

After cursing under his breath, he asks, "Why does this always happen?"

He grabs another one and this time, opens it a little bit more carefully.

"Robert, you really need to tell me what's going on. Where were you today?"

"I didn't see her today. I didn't know. I was at work, like I said. I slept there and I only got home two hours ago."

"Okay, good, so how did you ... Why did you decide that she was missing?"

"Elin called me. She told me that she couldn't find her and they had plans to meet up today. I don't know. It's all so jumbled."

"Robert, did you know about her appointment this morning?"

"What appointment?" He raises an eyebrow.

"The one with the doctor, the gynecologist?"

"No. She had an appointment?"

"Yes. She was going to go with Elin."

"Why?"

"I guess she suspected that she was pregnant."

I watch his expression carefully as I say that. He swallows hard and then shifts his jaw from one side to the other. Popping his collar, he throws his hoodie over his head.

It's something of a nervous tic of his, but what I don't know is whether he's nervous about this conversation or if he's a nervous person in general.

"So, you had no idea that she might be pregnant or that she might have thought that she was pregnant?"

"No. Of course not. Wait, she's pregnant?"

"No, I'm not saying that. We haven't talked to the doctor yet, but she had the appointment."

"Why didn't she just get one of those tests at the drugstore?" he asks.

"I don't know. I'm going to talk to Elin about it. Anyway, did you speak to her today at all on the phone or texts?"

"No."

"Is that something that's uncommon?"

He thinks about it for a moment.

"Ever since I started this job, things have been kind of off. We haven't been talking as much. I've been working a lot and I don't know, we just haven't made much time for each other. After this project is over, I want us to take a trip, but I hadn't brought it up to her yet."

"You haven't?"

"No," he says, shaking his head.

"Do you think that there's a chance that she just left?"

He considers that for a moment.

"I don't know."

"Can you tell me about what happened?" I continue to press for information. "You came home, and then what?"

"Well, nothing. I just came home and Elin called me and she was all frantic. Then I realized that I haven't talked to Karen since yesterday morning."

"So, you don't know when she got in from her trip?"

"No, it was late already. She was going to get in at like midnight. I talked to her at the beginning of the day when she was still at that conference, the one I didn't want her to go to."

"Tell me more about that."

"What do you want to know?" He shrugs.

"Anything you can think of."

Robert shakes his head, looks down at the floor, picks at the nail on his thumb with his index finger and says.

"I told you already, the thing about the MLMs. It's all crap. They make you go to these conferences. They cost a lot of money and, of course, you have to pay out of pocket. They make you believe that you're going to be successful, but that's all crap."

"So, you didn't think that Karen was capable of selling these things?"

"No, I'm not saying that. Not at all. She probably would have been a good salesperson in a bookstore or a boutique, even though she wasn't really into clothes, but *this*? No. I definitely don't want her to do that. We fought about it for a while, but she wanted to help out. She wanted to bring in some money and she didn't exactly want to get a regular job because of her writing."

He hesitates for a moment and then narrows his eyes and takes a step closer to me.

"She invested $4,000," he says in a gasp. "That's a lot more money than we had, so when she told me she was going to this conference, I knew it was going to cost another $600. I wasn't exactly happy, so I didn't really want to hear from her. I was working anyway and I just needed an excuse to get out of the house."

"You wouldn't have any sort of surveillance cameras outside?"

"No," Robert says, shaking his head. "What's the point? There are neighbors everywhere. I guess I never thought anything would happen."

"Okay. Thank you. I'll give you my card and we'll be in touch."

He sighs deeply and walks me over to the front door. I take one last look around. Nothing is out of place, except for that unusual story about the curtains, but then again, everything about this guy is a little bit unusual.

When Lenore and I walk downstairs, we review our notes.

"I guess he told us pretty much the same story," Officer Lenore says.

"So, he came home around 5:30 and then what? What exactly?" I ask.

"Elin called him and told him that she hadn't seen his wife. That's when he got worried."

"He waited a couple of hours and then they called us."

I lean against the railing downstairs. A few neighbors walk by and I stop them and introduce myself. I ask them about Karen Moore Kaslar; what kind of person was she, when was the last time they saw her?

The woman who lives downstairs with the freckles and the tank top, even though it's close to fifty degrees outside, lights a cigarette and says that she tried to sell her some candles for her multi-level marketing business.

"I thought that she was making them herself, but apparently not, so I'm glad I didn't buy them," she says with a smirk. "You know it's a pyramid scheme, right? I did Mary Kay back in the day and they're all the same."

"Okay. Is there anything else? Do you remember the last time that you saw her?" I ask, cutting her short.

"Like three days ago, standing out here with her suitcase, waiting for an Uber. She said she was going on a business trip, Phoenix, but that was it."

"You didn't hear anything today?"

"No. I was home all day," she says, shaking her head.

"No unusual sounds?"

"Like what?"

"I don't know, just anything out of the ordinary," I say.

"Are you ... Do you really ... Do you think that her husband did it?" she asks, pointing her cigarette in my face.

"I'm not saying that."

"Well, I guess he'd be the type, huh?"

"What do you mean?"

She runs her fingers through her thinning hair and takes another drag of a cigarette.

"I don't know. He just always seemed a little odd."

"How long have they lived here?" I ask.

"Three, four years, I think. I've been here like ten. My landlord isn't too happy about that."

I try to steer the conversation back to Robert.

"So, back to today, no unusual sounds?"

"Nope," she says, after thinking about it for a moment. "There was a lot of noise from the elementary school across the street, you know, all of their bells and all that stuff, but that's what happens usually on a weekday."

"Anything unusual?"

"No. Not that I can think of."

I nod my head and thank her for her time. Officer Lenore walks me to my car. We discuss the case, or the lack thereof, in a little more detail.

"Thanks for coming out," he says. "I wasn't sure what kind of report I was going to make, but that was good to see you in action."

"Yeah, of course. Do you want to be a detective someday?"

"Yeah, of course," he says with a smile, "but that's a lot of years in the future."

"Well, you never know. You just keep doing a good job and they might give you the opportunity."

"Is that what happened with you?"

"Yeah, sort of. I had this one case that kind of pushed me up a pay grade."

"Oh, yeah? What happened?"

My thoughts drift back to the docks near the Queen Mary, but I'm not ready to talk about it with a complete stranger just yet.

"I'll tell you about it some other time," I say. "I actually have to go deal with some personal issues right now."

"Oh, yes, of course. I heard about your sister."

I nod.

"Yeah. How is she? I mean, sorry." He fumbles over his words. "Is she still missing?"

"Yes, she is. Two days. It doesn't look great."

"Is there any chance that she ran away?"

"No." I shake my head. "She's thirteen and she's not the type. She's a good girl. She always called whenever she stayed out late, that kind of thing."

Then I think back to how she called me last summer and asked me to come get her. Even then, she told Mom where she was going.

"So, she just vanished?"

"She got dropped off by her friend's mom in front of the house, but she never walked in. I have no idea what could have happened. The mom was there with her friend and they dropped her off, so no one knows what happened."

"Wow, that's really scary."

"Yeah."

"What if she had plans to meet up with someone else?" Lenore asks. "Like a boyfriend."

"What do you mean?" I narrow my eyes, wanting to hear his thinking, his line of thought.

"No, nothing. I'm just talking."

"No, seriously. Tell me."

"I was just thinking back to being that age and I was dating this girl, but her parents were really strict. She used to tell them that she was hanging out with this one friend and she was really hanging out with me. That's what we used to do, just get around it, you know?"

"Yeah. I don't know. That may be the case. I thought that we were close and she would have told me about it. Maybe that could have been possible the first night, but she didn't come back yet and it's been a while."

"Yeah, I get it. That's not good. I'm sorry."

"Well, the good news, Lenore, is that you may have yourself the makings of a detective."

"Really?"

"Yep. You'd be surprised how few people would connect those dots in that way, so chin up. You might have a good career yet."

I get in the car and drive away from him, watching his face beam in the rearview mirror. My apartment is not too far away from here and as soon as I get in, I climb into the shower. I'm going to make the report later on tonight, but first I have to get back up to Big Bear.

***

WHEN I CLIMB out of the shower, I wrap myself in a towel and lie down on the bed.

My clothes are piled on the chair in the corner and there's one, sad, little plant that I have forgotten to water for close to a week. I know that I need to get back home as soon as possible to try to find my sister, but I don't know how much more time I can take off from work.

I snuck in these hours and I had to be back here to close a previous case, but I don't have that much time off. As a detective, I work long hours and the department does not look too keenly on people who take a lot of personal days off.

So far, they've been pretty understanding about my missing sister and the urgency of the matter, but the more days that click by, the less understanding they'll be.

No matter how much I insist that she's not the type to run away, a part of me wonders if she did. What if my bookworm, quiet, little girl of a sister had a secret life?

That's not even a what-if anymore. I know that's true. My mom doesn't, but the captain of the sheriff's station up there showed me what they found on her computer; videos of her friends in compromising situations.

She was there, recording it all. Why? I don't know.

For what purpose? I also don't know.

The one other thing I know is that the girl that she was supposedly not particularly friends with, but who appeared in that video, Natalie D'Achille, is now missing as well.

She was supposed to come home, and she didn't. At least that's what I heard from my mom. I need to get up there and talk to the captain to get all the details, but suddenly, I feel like there is a thick, damp blanket that has descended upon me that I can't lift off my body or free myself from.

I get on my side, lie down in the fetal position, and close my eyes. I know that all cops feel this way. Sometimes the work just gets to be too much. There's just too much darkness, too much pain, too much disappointment. In what other job do you constantly deal with everyone else's worst days?

Maybe if you're an emergency room doctor, but at least you can do something to help them. At least some of them survive.

I grab my phone and scroll aimlessly through social media, then I check my emails. There's nothing but spam and nothing really of interest.

I check my text messages again, wanting to see one from Luke, the FBI agent who it felt like I had a good connection with the last time that we were together, but nothing.

He had to go off on a job to Northern California and he said that he'd be in touch later that day, but I haven't heard much in a few days.

He's ghosting me. It's obvious, of course, but I still don't want to believe it. Some people would ask, "Why not just call me and tell me that you don't want to see me?" but I know the answer. They don't want the conflict. They don't want the trouble.

Besides, it's not like you don't really want to see this person again. Maybe it was just nothing to him, like just another day, just another date. I get it. You can't expect much from these one-off meetings, these one-off dates.

Sometimes you have a connection, sometimes you don't.

I'm used to it, of course. I've had plenty of dating experiences in all of these years of being single, but sometimes it's still nice to think that maybe the connection that you thought you made was real and the person on the other end felt the same way.

Oh, well.

My phone rings and I answer it just as I start to get ready. I put it on speakerphone.

"What's up, Sydney?" I ask.

She's my closest friend in the department and she was the one there with me that night when I met Luke.

"How are you? Just wanted to see what's new with your sister."

"Nothing. Violet is still missing and now this acquaintance of hers is also, so I guess they're going to give the case a little bit more priority, which I hope is good, but otherwise no news."

I've been keeping her abreast as to what's going on and she's been demanding text updates at least once every few hours. It's a little bit annoying, but it's nice to know that there's someone there actually giving a damn about me.

I start to pack my things. I grab the suitcase that I had before, and I throw in an extra pair of jeans and some warm sweaters. It's going to be cold up there in Big Bear Lake. Another blizzard is coming.

"Do you want me to come up with you? Maybe there's something I can do," she says. "I have a few days saved up."

"No, that's okay." I hesitate.

"Come on, let me help," she insists, and I don't want to say no again.

"When are you leaving?"

"As soon as I can," I say, grabbing my toiletries kit, the one that I hadn't even unpacked since I got back.

"Okay, half an hour. Is that good enough?"

"Yeah, that'd be great," I say, and she hangs up.

3

After I pack my things, I walk around my apartment trying to kill some time, trying to ease my mind, but nothing seems to work. I decide to put on my sneakers and go for a run. I've never been much of a gym kind of girl or even yoga. I've always found it a little bit too boring.

I like the way that exercise makes me feel, after the fact, but who doesn't, right? To actually get yourself out there and get that initial momentum going is pretty difficult though.

I put on some yoga pants, tie up my shoelaces, and change into a sports bra. I zip up my hoodie and grab my phone along with a pair of AirPods that I tend to wear whenever I'm alone. Am I the only one who does this? I like listening to podcasts, audiobooks, anything.

Sometimes I do need to let my mind just wander, but most of the time, it's nice to occupy my thoughts with something other than death, destruction, and sadness. I run down the stairs, around and out of the parking lot turning left on my street and gunning it all the way down to the next block. I get a stitch in my side by the time I get to the block after that and I slow down to a near jog.

"Great," I say to myself. I check my watch and it hasn't even been half a mile. "Okay, just keep going. You can do this."

I force myself to trot.

"Just lift up your feet one foot at a time. Keep going."

I wouldn't say that I am particularly out of shape, but I could stand to lose twenty pounds. Somehow over the years, my hips have become a little rounder and all of that snacking in the car has caught up with me. There was a time in my life back in college when I would go on a quick fast for two, three days and lose whatever excess fat managed to pile on over the summers. With age comes consequences, hormones, and things like that become difficult to deal with.

I'm not that old. I know that. So, I can't really use that as an excuse. I guess I'm just set in my ways. Whenever I'm a little bit stressed or go to do an interview, interrogation, or have an unpleasant interaction, I immediately grab something sweet to snack on to put me at ease.

I know I'm not the only one. Otherwise, obesity wouldn't be the epidemic that it is all around the world. About a mile into my run, I come to a complete stop and turn around to catch my breath.

I know that people say that you need time for yourself and use the time to meditate and take care of who you are in order to be healthier and happier. I never really understood that until just recently. Ever since I graduated from the University of Southern California, I've just been going in the same go, go, go mode. No breaks, no pauses, and no time for reflection, but that has to change.

I feel myself getting burnt out. Other people hit the wall much earlier and have given up the force altogether or switch to easier departments. I wanted to make detective. I wanted to grow. I wanted to devote my whole life to this. I have and I have succeeded.

So far, I'm pretty proud of what I've accomplished, but there's another part of me that thinks about some of the other things that I could have had, maybe should have had.

One thing is that I've always wanted to get a graduate degree. I've enjoyed learning my whole life and I know that there's so much more that I want to know. I'm not entirely certain of the field, but I'm interested in forensic psychology, criminology, or something along the lines that are related to my work. Of course, in order to fit that in, I have to actually make more time in my schedule.

What are the other things that I'm interested in? Settling down. I hate the cliché, of course, but I've spent so much of my life trying to run away from being that typical girl. I don't like to show my feelings. I have embedded myself in a field where toxic masculinity rules and tends to dominate everything we do, the good and the bad. I know that I have something to offer. Not just as a detective, but also as a woman and yeah, I guess it would be nice to have a partner.

I've dated a lot, had a few men break my heart, and there were a few of them that I thought that I could have a future with, but things never worked out.

What was the problem? Work. I have to work around their schedules, but when it came to my career and my obligations, they didn't seem to want to work around mine at all.

My thoughts go back to Luke.

I met him while working on my last case and he was a rebound guy for me after what happened with my ex. I wasn't looking to date anyone, and I definitely wasn't looking to get involved with anyone romantically. Then things progressed.

I like him a lot. He works for the FBI and though I swore that I wasn't going to date any more men in law enforcement, I couldn't stop myself.

Well, hell, I'm getting ahead of myself. Date is not exactly the right word.

We saw each other a few times. Spend the night and had amazing sexual chemistry. Then he had to go up to Northern California for work. He has texted a few times, but we haven't spoken on the phone and he hasn't asked me about my sister much.

I get the feeling that he's ghosting me and well, that's just how modern relationships unfold, right?

Why tell someone that you're actually not interested in them when you can just text a little bit, a few words here and there, promise to call, and then never do?

Is that such a modern thing after all though? Isn't that something that people who have avoided personal conflict have always done? We just finally have a word for it.

"Hey. Kaitlyn? Is that you? Kaitlyn Carr?"

I stop mid-jog and I feel my body recoil against nothing in particular.

"Hi," I say, feeling my cheeks with the back of my hands. They're on fire. I gasp for some air and try to desperately get a good amount in without much luck.

"I can't believe it's you," he says, opening the top button of his expensive suit to drape his arm around my shoulder.

I bend myself in half to try to get some more air and partly to try to die a little from the embarrassment.

Is this really him? No, no, no, it can't be him. Go away. This isn't happening. Why the heck did I ever go on this run?

I stand up straight, exhaling slowly and then quickly suck in some more air.

"Hi." I plaster a fake smile on my face.

"Hi," he says, tilting his head.

His hair has a perfect fade on the side and it's long out in the front with a strand falling into his eyes. There's a light right above us illuminating his strong jawline and his strands of sand. I watch him lick his lips, luscious and thick, just the way I remember them. I slowly let my eyes meet his piercing green eyes, the color of spring grass.

"I can't believe it's you," he says, taking a step away from me.

I lift up my arm and wipe the sweat off my brow. I couldn't look less attractive if I tried. I glance down at my shirt and see big dark pit stains. My hair is stringy and oily, pulled up into a haphazard bird's nest on top of my head. I don't remember if I'm wearing any makeup, but it's the end of the day and if I were wearing some, it's probably all gone by now.

"Mark?"

"You recognize me, right?"

"Yeah, of course," I say a little bit too quickly. "Mark Benioff. So, what are you doing here?"

"Oh, I have a client," he says, "just right over there. We're meeting up at Fig & Olive to sign a deal."

"Huh," I say, trying to hide my surprise, but finding that an impossibility.

Fig & Olive is one of the fanciest restaurants in West Hollywood and it's the type of place where presidents go to raise money for their new foundations and where senators go to raise money for their reelection campaigns. I've never been there. The entrees go for almost seventy dollars a plate, if not more.

"Are you okay?" Mark asks, reaching over and touching my hand again.

"Yeah, I'm sorry. How are you? What's going on? I didn't even know that you were in LA."

"No, I'm not very active on social media," he says with a shrug. The confidence is just oozing out of his pores and I feel whatever confidence I had in me suddenly decrease by a metric ton.

"Yeah, okay. I get that," I say.

"Actually, I saw on Facebook that you're now a detective." I don't know if he meant to bring up my own social media presence, or not to throw it in my face, but I let it slide.

"Yeah, I am," I say. "LAPD."

"Wow. Congratulations."

"I've been doing it for a few years now. How about you?"

"Defense attorney."

"Oh, really?" I ask, surprised. "I didn't even know that you went to law school."

"Well, you and I haven't really talked *since*."

Don't say it. Don't say it. Don't say it, I say silently to myself and he doesn't.

"Where did you go to law school?"

"San Diego," he says. "I just needed to get out of town."

"Yeah, I get it. How long have you been doing that?"

"Oh, I lived there for many years and then decided to move up. I have a place in Santa Monica now."

I try to calculate in my head how long it has been since I've seen Mark. Twelve years I guess and the last time I talked to him was probably eight years ago.

I don't know what else to say. I keep looking at him and how pretty he is. Suddenly, I'm thrown back to junior year and that trip to Hawaii that started it all.

"Hey, would you like to go and get something to eat sometime?"

"Yeah, I guess. Sure," I say with a nod. The words just come out of my mouth as if on their own without my consent and I regret that immediately, but I can't very well take them back.

"Well, listen, I have to go. My client is waiting. I'd love to grab a drink, catch up. Whatever."

I nod. "Okay. You look great by the way."

"Thanks. You do, too."

I watch him walk away. The suit is loose-fitting, but his ass is still as fit and round as it was back then. Maybe even better. I growl to myself and spin around on my heels.

4

"Hey, I've been waiting for you forever," Sydney says, getting up from the stoop. She has her small suitcase with her. The screen of her phone is turned on and she gestures with it to draw her point home.

"Sorry, I thought that I had time to go on a short run before you got here."

"Wow, look at you," Sydney says, tossing her hair from one side to the other. "I guess you're really sticking to this exercise thing, huh?"

"I don't know." I walk past her and up the stairs and still try to process seeing Mark.

"Wait, what's going on? What happened? Something wrong with Violet?"

"No, no. No news about Violet," I say and suddenly feel a pang of guilt over the fact that I haven't thought about my missing sister in half an hour.

I open the door, welcome her inside, and head straight to the shower.

"I'll be just a few minutes," I say, dropping my clothes on the floor behind the closed door.

I run the water, get in, and as soon as I close the door to the shower, Sydney opens the one to the bathroom.

"Okay, what's going on? Something is off," she announces and looks at herself in the mirror. It's hard to believe that this woman has a master's degree from UCLA and works as a homicide detective yet still has the ability to morph into a ditzy thirty-year-old girl with an Instagram personality when she pretends to be on social media.

Of course, there's no mention of her life as a detective on there, just pictures of her posing in front of different walls and ice cream shops, as well as the obligatory close-ups of Starbucks coffee cups.

"Your extensions look nice," I say, washing my hair knowing full well that I probably won't get the chance to do this again for at least a day or two.

"Yeah, I just got them today. What do you think?"

"I told you that I like them."

"Yeah, I'm not so sure. They're quite heavy. Have you ever had extensions?"

"No. They seem like too much work."

"Well, who am I talking to? You don't even fucking... You don't even color your hair at a salon. What are you doing? Still doing it on your own?"

I shake my head and respond, "Okay, listen, I told you that when I was drunk and we were sharing. I don't want you to throw it in my face every time. You want to make me feel bad about something."

"Oh, honey. No, not at all," she says, popping her collar and applying a fresh coat of lipstick to her thick, luscious lips.

After a few minutes, I stop the water and get out.

"How are you done already?" Sydney asks. "The mirror isn't even fogged up."

"Well, that's not really a requirement," I joke and wrap a towel around myself.

"So, what happened? What's wrong?"

I use another towel to dry off and wrap it around my hair.

"I ran into Mark."

"What?" Her mouth makes a big O sound and she enunciates with her next word, "Seriously?"

"Yeah, seriously."

"Oh my god. Tell me everything."

I go over every single detail that I remember no matter how embarrassing. She listens with her mouth slightly ajar hanging on every word.

"He wants you back," she announces.

"No, I just feel like such an idiot. I can't believe that after all this time, I see him and I'm not dressed up to the nines looking amazing, but instead I'm looking like this. It's so embarrassing and he looked so handsome."

I hate admitting that, but with Sydney, I can't lie about something like that.

"His hair was in a fade. It was all perfect. A little bit of gel, but not too much. I don't know, he looked like, he looks like a movie star. It's ridiculous."

"Okay, don't feel bad. If he was acting the way that you said that he was acting, then he's clearly so into you."

"I don't want him to be into me. I just want him to, I don't know."

"What? What do you want?"

I walk past her and into my bedroom. I put on a pair of loose-fitting jeans that will work for a three-hour car ride up the mountain as well as a long sleeve shirt and the most comfortable bra that I own.

"I don't know. I don't know what I want," I say, taking my hair down and brushing it out.

"You really shouldn't brush your hair wet," she says. "It causes breakage."

"Okay, but then it dries in all these different directions and I can't have that."

"Oh, you just let it air dry?"

"Yes. I don't like hair dryers."

"Oh my God. How does your hair even look so nice?" she asks, crossing her hands and sitting down on the edge of the couch. "I had no idea you did this. So, what is it that you do exactly?"

I glare at her and question, "Are you seriously asking me about my hair when I just told you that I ran into my ex-boyfriend, the one that I was engaged to and the one that you now say may or may not want me back?"

"Yes. Have you seen your hair? It looks amazing. I thought you blow dried every morning."

"No, maybe it looks amazing because I don't. I wash it at night whenever I can as soon as I get off my shift. It usually dries by the time I go to bed. Whichever crinkly part appears, I straighten that out with the straightener in the morning."

"Oh my God." Her mouth drops open, shocked, maybe appalled.

"Okay, can we focus? This is devolving into some other conversation that I really don't want to have right now."

"Okay, okay. I'm focused," she says, blinking her eyes. "Mark, Mark Benioff. I remember him."

"You never even met him."

"I remember you telling me about him, and I remember the way that you talked about him. It kind of made it seem like you weren't really over him."

"Over him? It's been twelve years. Of course, I'm over him."

"Do you ever think about him?"

"I don't know. Maybe."

"Then you're not over him."

"That's a really low standard. Of course, most people think about their ex-girlfriends at some point in their lives or ex-boyfriends, right? You see their picture on social media, you reminisce a little bit. There's nothing wrong with that."

"Show me his picture."

"Well, that's the thing. I don't have any. I have the ones from back then, but he says that he's not on social media anymore or hasn't been. Whatever. I don't know. He made it seem like it was something vain and then, of course, he also mentioned that he had looked me up and I just feel like such an idiot."

"Okay, don't," she says, putting her finger in my face. "Please don't. You're not an idiot. You're just feeling insecure. It happens. We all feel like that. You didn't see him looking your best and whatever. Besides, you don't want to see him again, right?"

"Well, that's the thing," I say, shifting my weight from one foot to another, putting on a thick pair of boots. "I kind of promised. He asked me if I wanted to go do something and I said I did."

"What, dinner?"

"Well, first he mentioned dinner, but then he brought up drinks, so I'm not exactly sure."

I tell her about how we should bring our suitcases or small overnight bags to my car and I let her park in my spot.

"How long is this trip for anyway?" she asks. "I have to be at work on Thursday morning. Should I take my own car?"

"I don't know exactly. I have my next shift tomorrow night so that's probably as long as I can get unless I can get an extension. Do you want to take your own car?"

"No. Let's drive up together. I'll figure out something if you need to stay longer."

"Okay, thanks."

5

O n the drive up, we listen to a lot of music and eat a lot of pretzels that we buy at the gas station right before we start ascending up the mountain. I'm tempted to pass, I want to, but when I see her crunching on them, I can't say no. The anxiety and the built-up energy that I felt earlier in my apartment seems to dissipate a little bit as I drink in the hot mint tea that I refilled at the gas station and let the slightly salted pretzels melt in my mouth.

Sydney relaxes a little bit, too, and the mood becomes a little bit more somber.

"What happened with Mark back then?" she asks.

I can't remember what details of the story I've told her previously and I want to talk about something else, but I'd be lying if I said that my thoughts didn't keep coming back to him.

"We met at a party when I first got to USC," I say, biting my lower lip and keeping my eyes on the road with nothing but trees whizzing by me and the occasional flood of headlights. "I wasn't really big into parties, but my roommates invited me to this one and I don't remember why, but I just went. It was at an apartment building across from mine."

"So, this was what? Junior year?" she asks.

"Yeah, I transferred from Columbia. I was there for two years and I was having a lot of issues with my mom and I don't know, I had to fly back all the time from New York, and I really didn't like it as much as I thought I would."

"You didn't like New York?" Sydney asks.

"No. I don't know. Maybe it was a weird brainwashing thing that happened. I watched too many movies, too many shows about people going to New York and just becoming these super versions of themselves and I wanted that after growing up with my mom and everything that I went through with her. I don't know, I needed to go somewhere different. LA would have been far enough and maybe I should have just gone there right from the beginning, but I got into Barnard College. It's like the women's college associated with Columbia University and you can take classes at either institution. So, I went there. I had never been to New York before. I never even took a tour because my mom didn't really see the point of visiting colleges."

"Wait, what?" Sydney asks. "Different colleges have different fields and different social lives. You don't always fit into what the school offers."

"Yeah, I know that now, but I didn't know that then. My mom didn't think like that and I didn't really, I don't know, think like that either at that time. I was just seventeen.

"Anyway, to make a long story even longer, my mom kept calling me about all the problems she was having and just feeling me out about different things with Violet. She just didn't want me up there and I just decided that it'd be easier if I was in LA to just deal with everything instead of flying back and forth. Like I said before, I didn't really like New York as much as I thought I would."

"You thought you were going to be what? Like *Sex in the City* girls living it up?"

"Yeah. I know. It's stupid. The problem is that I wasn't in my thirties and I didn't have any money. I couldn't even afford to go to the movies."

"You're a girl, you could have guys buy drinks for you."

"Yeah, but then you have to talk to those guys. You have to have boring conversations about their boring lives, and I didn't want to deal with that."

"Someone might say that's kind of your problem," Sydney says. "You just write every guy off and you don't give them a chance."

"Anyway, let's not talk about my sad love life. Let me tell you about Mark." I turn my attention back to the road and lose myself in the memories. "We met at this party. I was bored, drinking by the punch bowl waiting for something exciting to happen. My roommates immediately left me and found guys to talk to. I was just about to go home, but he caught up with me by the front door and just said, 'Hi, I'm Mark and I think you're cute.'"

"Wow. Just like that? Right off the bat?"

"Yeah, just like that. It's silly. Guys sometimes. It's hard making the first move and just putting yourself out there like that, but he just did, and he wasn't even drunk. I don't think he had a drink at all. He was just coming in and he saw me and said that. I told him that I'd talk to him for one drink. I remember that he ended up drinking it very, very slowly."

"Really?"

"Yeah. On purpose. When I called him on it, he said that he wanted to make the moment last as long as possible."

"Oh my god, that's so… swoon-worthy," Sydney says.

I smile and blush even though it's pitch black, but I feel my cheeks get red.

"So, what happened?"

"That whole semester we were just together all the time. He'd meet me after class, walk me to my next class. I'd meet him after his labs, and he had this one really long art class that was like four hours long. We always had Chinese food afterward and we studied together at Doheny."

"Doheny?"

"The library there. We made out in the stacks more than a few times."

"Ooh, sexy. What happened? Why aren't you and Mark together forever having lots of babies?"

"Lots of babies?" I smirk and look at her. "Aren't you just engaged? Don't act like you don't know what happens to college boyfriends."

"Okay, yes, but honestly, I've never had a college boyfriend like that. You guys sound so cute and perfect like out of a romantic comedy."

"Yeah, we were inseparable, but then I went to meet his parents and things were just off. They're really Catholic. There was a whole situation where I went to visit his sister in Northern California. They'd just moved into a new house, but there was not enough room for everyone to stay there. So, we got a hotel room, but his parents insisted on sort of getting everyone hotel rooms and paying for them so that everyone could be together in the same hotel. Then they found out that we were planning on staying in the same room together and they freaked out. They kept insisting that I had to stay in the room by myself because Mark was going to stay in a room with his brother. That was the same night that I first met them and it was just so awkward and weird. Mark got really mad and yelled at them. We stayed in the same room, but it was just the whole weekend was really off after that."

"Yeah, I imagine, but what does that have to do with what happened between you and Mark?"

"I don't know. The thing with his family didn't exactly work out, and then he was really close to them, and it just felt like our relationship was sort of causing problems."

"Okay, I feel like I'm pulling teeth. What happened?"

"I had to go to Hawaii for this conference. I was a physics major. I don't even remember what the conference was about, but I was doing a presentation from this research that I'd done in class and he was going to go with me. It was a school/fun trip combination thing, but then last minute, he just said that he couldn't go and we got into this fight. I really wanted him to come because I was really scared of doing this presentation and it just felt like I honestly didn't know anything about physics in comparison to everyone else who was going to be there. Anyway, he said that he had this term paper to work on that he had been slacking off and it was due right after the conference. That was true. Although, I didn't want to understand and I went alone, we were in a fight. At one point, we both talked about basically taking a break from one another. I don't know, I guess to some degree we broke up. I don't know. It's just one of those confusing times and I felt like we broke up.

"I was really upset. I was crying the whole flight to Hawaii. It was my first time there and everyone was so happy. These people greeted us with these leis and I was just bawling. It was just awful. Anyway, I called him later that night even though I knew that we had broken up, but I wanted to talk, I just didn't really want to accept it. I thought that maybe things could be different and we could work on it."

I suck in some air and exhale quickly, but it doesn't make the pain of remembering what happened any easier. Sydney waits for me to continue. She doesn't prod any more. She knows that the inevitable is coming, but just not about the details of what that means exactly.

I smack my lips realizing just how long I've been talking and how dry my mouth has gotten. I take a swig of my tea which is no longer hot, but more like a tepid, room temperature water that tastes like mint.

"I called him and this girl answered. When I asked her who she was or where Mark was, she said that he was in the bathroom."

"That's it?" Sydney asks. "That's all he did?"

"He called me back later that night a bunch of times, but I was really angry. I was so pissed. Like, who the hell does he think he is? Why is he with her already? Why did he have to ruin this wonderful thing that we had? So, I went out with a bunch of my conference friends, we went out to dinner and then to drinks, at this club, I met a guy."

"Oh my God."

"Yeah. He was cute and he was a marine. We made out and I don't know, I just took him home with me and we slept together."

"Oh my God. What about that girl that Mark was with?"

"I talked to him finally a couple of days into the conference and he was really sorry. He was so upset. Apparently after we broke up, he went out with a few friends and met her and did the same thing that I'd done."

"Really? Kaitlyn? It's not like you cheated on each other, you were already broken up."

"Yeah, I know, but I don't know. He told me that and I was really hurt. I told him what I did and obviously he was really hurt. We were just both so angry and so prideful, we just called it quits for good. I haven't talked to him since."

"Not at all?"

"Nope, not at all. I've heard about him through some friends. I had Facebook and other social media so I'm sure he could have found out stuff about me like he did. He mentioned that he knew I'd joined the LAPD and I don't know, just general stuff like that. Since he wasn't on social media, I didn't know anything about him. We haven't talked since that breakup. I haven't seen him either, until just today."

We drive for a while. I let that sink in, that whole story of this man that used to mean the world to me and how stupidly it all ended. I know that I was too proud and he was, too, and we were hurt also, but looking back on it, I think about all the years that we missed because of that series of mistakes that we made.

I don't know the man that Mark is now and I'm sure that I have changed a lot, too, but I remember the way that we were together and how much everything made sense. How I had this person with me who supported me no matter what, who was there for me. I know that we weren't together very long. Five months is probably more accurate. Regardless, the time that we had spent together and the depths to which we got to know each other meant a lot.

"So, do you know if he's married or with anybody now?" Sydney asks as we pull up to my mom's house.

I shake my head.

"You don't know anything?"

"No, I don't know anything."

"What about you? Does he know that you're single?"

"Sydney." I turn off the engine and look at her. "Listen, nothing's going to happen. We just ran into each other. We had a good time and maybe it's one of those relationships that shouldn't have ended when it ended, but it's all in the past. It was nice to see him. I wish that I hadn't looked the way I looked, but yeah. It was nice to see him and I'd like to meet up and catch up with him again, but can we not talk about this anymore? This is ancient history, okay?"

"Okay," she says.

We get out of the car.

6

s soon as my mom opens the door, she throws a smile on her face and reaches out to hug Sydney as tightly as possible.

"Oh, you shouldn't have come, but thank you. Thank you so much for being here."

Sydney has met my mom on a few occasions and I've always known that Mom has a soft spot for her. I'm glad that she's happy to see her.

"Sorry I didn't warn you about bringing anyone."

"No, don't worry about it. Sydney is welcome here anytime, even when you're not," Mom jokes, but we all know that's only a half truth. "Well, I made dinner, but not for three. I have plenty of food. So, we're all set."

She throws her arms out to the spread that she has laid out on the dining room table.

"Oh, wow. I'm surprised," I say, putting my bag down and taking off my coat. I take Sydney's coat and put it on the peg near the front door where all of the winter gear goes. We take off our shoes while sitting on the bench and tuck them neatly underneath.

The dining room table, which is right to the left of the front door is covered with different plates of food: macaroni and cheese, canned cranberries, a pumpkin pie, Hot Pockets, mushroom and spinach pizza, along with an assortment of breads, banana and pumpkin being the most prominent.

"Mom. Why, why do you have all this food?"

"Well, I realized the last time that you were here, I really should have been a better hostess and mom."

"Come on, what's going on?" I ask.

"I'm just nervous, you know, and I needed to do something. So, I just got a bunch of food and heated it up. I thought that we could have a really extensive meal kind of like Thanksgiving, but not Thanksgiving. You know, just to take our minds off things or to refuel. It's very important to refuel, girls. You two have very busy lives and I want you to take care of yourselves. Work isn't all that there is."

"Yes. I know, Mrs. Carr," Sydney says, waving her left hand demonstratively.

When Mom's eyes focus on her engagement ring, she lets out a little squeal and rushes over to look at her hand.

"You're engaged to that nice boy, Patrick Flannery, right, Sydney? Right?"

"Oh my God. You know his name?"

"Yeah. Kaitlyn told me all about him, FBI, right? Very nice."

"Actually, Kaitlyn..." Sydney starts to say as our eyes meet and I shake my head.

I don't know whether she's about to bring up Mark, my ex-boyfriend who my mom is all too well familiar with, or Luke, the FBI agent that I met when I was out with Sydney the last time, but I don't want to talk about either of them.

"Well, all of this food looks wonderful," Sydney says, taking a seat across from me.

Mom sits at the head of the table as usual. I glance down and see that there are even placemats and plates. Mom quickly creates a place for Sydney right across from me.

"You really made all this food just for the two of us?" I ask.

"I wanted to do something nice," she finally says and takes a sip of her wine.

I reach over and pour some wine into my and Sydney's glasses. We all clink and have an unspoken moment of silence for Violet. I swallow hard as I feel tears welling up at the back of my eyes. I know that I have to say something to make the pain go away.

"Thank you for coming Sydney," I say, raising my glass once again. "I really appreciate you supporting both of us during this difficult time. I know that we need all the help that we can get in finding her."

"You will, you will find her," Sydney says, reaching over and giving me a firm squeeze.

"Okay, I need some good news," Mom says. "Tell me about your engagement."

Sydney smiles and she starts with, "Well, his name is Patrick, but you already know that. He works for the FBI and we met on a case. He had a little bit of a big head and I put him in his place."

"Ooh, I like that," Mom says, giving me a wink. "How long have you been together?"

"About a year."

"How did he ask you to marry him?"

"It was a surprise. I actually didn't see it coming at all."

"Really? What happened?" Mom asks.

"We were walking by Santa Monica pier and he put his arms around me and then told me he loved me. I gave him a kiss. He pulled away and got down on one knee. He said he was going to wait until there was a special moment, but why wait? This was it. He told me he loved me and that he wanted to spend the rest of his life with me."

"Oh my God, Sydney. That's amazing. Congratulations." Mom reaches over and squeezes her hand.

I take a few bites of my food and then another sip of wine. Mom licks her lips and looks directly at me, our eyes meet for a moment and then mine dart away. I stare at the collection of plates hanging on the other side of the dining room. They're collector's items though, with little blue flowers and intricate designs on them. My mom has had them forever and frankly, I don't even remember when she started to collect them. Every few years, a new one pops up. I keep meaning to ask her about it, but I never do.

"Tell me about those plates," I say, trying to change the topic.

"Oh, I'm glad you finally noticed. For a detective you're not particularly observant."

"Ha, ha," I say with a tinge of sarcasm. "You think you're so funny?"

"Well, I started collecting those plates back in the seventies. I got the first one at a thrift store down on Wilcox Avenue and then whenever I find another one, whenever it's part of a set, I get it."

"They're beautiful," Sydney says, even though I know that she's lying. She hates things like this, kitschy and old-fashioned.

"I think they're made in the sixties by a porcelain company, but I can't be too sure. The print on the back is usually worn off."

I'm about to say something about how if the print is gone, then it's probably not porcelain, but I decide to keep my mouth shut.

"So, what about you, Kaitlyn?" Mom says, taking a bite, putting a large helping of mac and cheese on her plate.

"What about me?"

"Dating anyone new?"

"No."

"I know that things didn't exactly work out with Thomas and I'm sorry about that." Mom knew that we dated for a while, but not all of the details of the breakup. "It would have been nice to meet him."

"Mom, we didn't date long enough for that," I say, grabbing a slice of banana bread.

You'd think that having this convoluted dinner with all the various types of food combinations wouldn't be good, but actually it reminds me a little bit of a buffet I had in Vegas. You pick what you want, and you get to have a lot of bad things all at once. The banana bread is fresh and it practically melts in my mouth.

"Yeah, Thomas wasn't that great, Mrs. Carr," Sydney says, "but this new guy, he's got some potential."

"There is no potential," I say, shaking my head.

"Of course there is."

"You had a few dates with Luke, right? You liked him, right?" Sydney nudges me, kicking my foot under the table. I want to roll my eyes, but I hope that my expression is enough.

"Nothing is happening with Luke. I haven't heard from him in a couple of days," I say.

"So what?"

"Well, he's either busy on a case, though I don't see why he still can't text me or ask about my missing sister at least sporadically or he's just not interested."

"I thought you had a good connection?" Sydney says.

"Yeah, I thought so, too, but I guess not."

She nods and I nod as well.

I finish my glass of wine and pour myself another. We sit here for a little bit, enjoying our food and saying nothing at all. I expect my mom to ask me more about Luke, but she doesn't and for that, I'm thankful.

Instead, I let my thoughts go back to Violet and for this, I'm not thankful. It seems like whenever there's a lull in conversation or anytime that I can be alone with myself, I think about her.

Of course, being in this house isn't helping much. There are reminders of her everywhere.

After we finish dinner and are too full for dessert, Sydney and I clear the table while we force my mom to go sit down in the recliner in the living room and just take it easy. When I put the food away in the fridge, I see Violet's report card on the front, along with some drawings that she'd made.

"Straight As?" Sydney asks. "Wow. I didn't think that they sent out report cards anymore. I thought that was a relic of the past, like taxi cabs and taking notes on paper."

"Yeah, I don't think they do, but Mom always printed out mine and now she has even more of a reason to be proud, so she's been printing out Violet's."

"Your sister has gotten straight As ever since she was in first grade and she probably would've gotten straight As in preschool, too, but they didn't grade people then!" Mom yells from the living room.

I chuckle and say, "Yeah, she was a straight A student."

"What about you?" Sydney asks.

"Me? No. I was not much of one, not much of a student."

"How did you get into USC?"

"Well, okay, I wasn't much of a student until high school. I guess I did okay in elementary school, but middle school years were a little bit dark."

"Oh, did you tell your friend about how you used to alter your report cards?" Mom yells.

"No, I didn't. I'm not sure that's something that you should notify people of who work in law enforcement," I say.

"Oh, come on, you can tell me." Sydney laughs. "You used to fake your report cards?"

"Yeah. I used to go to the library, photocopy them, and put in different grades."

"Photocopy them?"

"Yeah, it was really primitive because they would still come in the mail, so I would just photocopy part of it and then put a little piece of paper over the C or B and change it to an A. Mom caught onto it after a while."

"Well, you can only see so many photocopied report cards before you get suspicious."

I feel my cheeks get flushed.

"I didn't think that I was going to come here and relive every embarrassing moment from my childhood," I say.

"Hey, I thought we were all friends," Mom jokes. "If you come over here, Sydney, I'll show you some of her old yearbooks."

"Yes, of course!" Sydney yells, leaving me alone with the dishes.

We don't have a dishwasher, so I wash each one by hand. I don't really mind. I actually find the process quite soothing. I had a dishwasher in one of the apartments I lived in a while ago, but it always required you to basically wash off all of the dishes prior to putting them in there and so I always thought of that as tripling the work. Why not just scrub it one or two additional times and put it on the drying rack rather than into the dishwasher, wait for it to get done, then unload the dishwasher? Blah, blah, blah, too many steps for me.

It takes me a while to get through all the plates because, in addition to the ones we used, I also have to move all of the food to the storage containers and put them in the refrigerator, Mom's orders. Finally, after drying my hands with a towel, I plop down on the sunken couch that desperately needs to be either reupholstered or just thrown away.

I see that my mom wasn't kidding about the yearbooks. She has each one from every year that I was in school and they are meticulously going through them.

"Instead of that, let's try to be a little bit more productive and at least look at *Violet's* yearbooks," I suggest.

"You're only making that suggestion because you don't want me to see you in eighth grade with pimples all over your face," Sydney says, flipping over the book that she has been looking at and showing me a picture of myself in a track uniform, bent in half after finishing a two-mile run.

"Perfect. Yeah, this is useful," I mutter to myself.

"Kaitlyn, sometimes life isn't just about being useful. Sometimes it's about other things as well," Mom says, "like enjoying yourself. When was the last time you took a few moments to really smile?"

"I can't do that, Mom. I'm a homicide detective, remember?"

"You're more than that. I know that I raised a girl who was confident, outgoing, and positive. That's not who I see before me."

I stare at her and suddenly the tone of the conversation shifts.

"What are you talking about?" I ask.

"Don't you remember all the fun we used to have putting together scrapbooks and planning trips?"

"Planning trips that we never took? Is that what you're talking about?"

"Okay, just because they didn't work out doesn't mean that it was a wasted effort."

"Well, yeah, that's exactly what it means."

She made me put together poster boards of vacations and trips that we were going to take, but we never did. So, what exactly was the point of that, besides just getting my hopes up before having them all crash down?

"Kaitlyn, you've really changed, ever since you have become a detective, I feel like there's this negativity that surrounds you."

I shake my head in disbelief.

"Is this really happening?" I ask.

"Okay, let's not talk about that." Sydney tries to mediate.

"I'm sorry if my life isn't what you thought it would be," I say, "but that's how it works out sometimes. Guess what? It wasn't my dream to grow up knowing that my father was murdered."

"You shut up." Mom throws her finger in my face.

She's wearing a bracelet with a nautical symbol on it and it makes a loud jingling sound as her finger trembles but remains steadfast.

"Your father committed suicide and you know that. I don't know why you have to bring him up now, of all times."

I bite my lower lip and shake my head. All of this time and she still won't admit it. Sydney looks at me, her eyes like two big saucers.

"I'll tell you later," I say, crossing my arms in a huff.

Frankly, I don't know why I brought my father up at a time like this. I guess because I was a little bit angry at the fact that she was out here pretending that I had this perfect childhood and perfect life when things have always been pretty messed up, even before Violet went missing.

"No. She won't tell you anything true," Mom snaps. "My husband committed suicide. Kaitlyn came home and found him with a gunshot in his abdomen."

"Two," I correct her, putting my fingers up in the air. "Two shots."

"Why does that matter?"

"It matters because people don't commit suicide with two gunshots, Mom."

"Don't talk back to me, young lady," she snaps and turns her attention to Sydney. "My husband committed suicide, okay? Kaitlyn was very young. I'm sorry that I had a bit of a breakdown that day and I couldn't stop you from walking in there, but that doesn't change the fact that he did this terrible thing and we all have to live with it now. Your father was a very selfish man."

"He was not selfish, Mom."

"He was a drug addict and a drug dealer. He sold narcotics to make money. You of all people should know just what kind of selfishness it requires to do something like that."

"I'm not excusing his behavior and I know that he was a dealer. He sold them at my school. That doesn't change the fact that he did not kill himself. He *would not* kill himself."

"I know that's difficult for you to believe, honey," she gets up and sits down next to me, taking my hand in hers, "but your father had a lot of demons. He had a lot of things that he had to get over and deal with. I'm sorry that you still have trouble accepting that after all of these years but that's the truth, God's honest truth. Now this conversation is over," she says, reaching over and kissing me on the cheek.

Afterward, she gets up and walks away, holding her shoulders with her hands. I can see her whole body tremble as she disappears into the bedroom where I found my father.

The one where nothing has changed since his death, except for the change of sheets and the spot where he had bled onto the carpet. Same headboard, same furniture, same curtains, same everything.

A few months ago, when my mom was at work, I had to go and look for some of her clothes and I reached into her closet to look for a sweatshirt. That's when I saw that all of my father's old clothes are still there all these years later.

I just couldn't believe it. She didn't get rid of anything. There's barely enough room for her own stuff and yet his occupies the left-hand side of the closet, just like it always did.

"I'm sorry about that," I say to Sydney. "I don't know what came over me."

"It's okay. Families are complicated."

"Yeah." I nod, moving my jaw from one side to another. "I shouldn't have said that, but it's not true what she says either. I just got upset by the fact that she seems to have this whole other view of what my life was like growing up and it's just not true."

"Maybe that's just how she wants to remember it, maybe it's easier that way."

"I'm sure it is, but it's not easier on me. I want her to admit that I didn't have it that great and she could've done better, but I don't think she ever will."

"I don't think she can, Kaitlyn," Sydney says, shaking her head.

"What do you mean?"

"I don't think she can admit something like that, especially not now, but if she hasn't already, it would mean admitting that she's done something wrong. It would mean admitting that her life has been a lie and she wasn't a great mother. For some people that's really hard, especially if she tried at all and I guess she did."

I wait a few minutes and, after I feel like my mom has had enough time to properly cool off, I whisper to Sydney to wish me luck and then knock on her door.

7

"**M**om, can I talk to you?" I ask when she doesn't respond.

I knock again and again. Finally, I just reach for the doorknob and open the door. I find Mom sitting on the bed with her knees tucked up to her chest and her Kindle in front of her. The room is dark and her face is illuminated just from the light of her e-book.

"I'm sorry for bringing all that up," I say.

"I notice that you're not apologizing for saying any of it," Mom says without looking at me.

Her face is washed in blue light and suddenly she looks a few decades younger. Almost the same age as I am.

I don't know how to respond. In fact, I know how I want to respond, but I don't know if I can.

"Listen, we have something important to talk about, tomorrow's press conference. A lot of people are going to be there."

"Yeah, I know. I was waiting to see how long it'd take you to bring it up. I thought we were having a nice dinner."

"I thought that we were having fun."

"Having fun?" Mom reaches over and flips on the light next to the bed. Suddenly she's back to being her old self. "I'm not having fun while my daughter is missing, Kaitlyn."

"Okay, I don't know what the right word for it is, but I thought you were having a nice time and I wanted to have you enjoy yourself."

"I'm not enjoying myself while my daughter is missing, Kaitlyn, or is it Detective Carr?"

"What are you even talking about? Why are you getting so upset?"

"I don't know why you have to bring up your father at a time like this. You know that we disagree, and you know that it's better if we don't talk about it, so just leave bygones, be bygones or however that saying goes."

I inhale and exhale slowly, trying to choose my words carefully.

"Okay, we have the press conference tomorrow morning at nine o'clock. I think it's better if we get there at eight thirty at the latest to prepare."

"Prepare for what?"

"You have to make a speech. You have to appeal to the public. Do you know what you're going to say?"

"No," Mom says. "I thought you were going to do it."

"I guess I can."

"Come on, you have to, what am I going to say to them?"

"It's your daughter who's missing. I think it would be best if we both talk. The more human we appear, the more interest the case will spark."

"Human? Do we not appear human now?"

"After that display at dinner, I'm not so sure, Mom." The sarcastic remark escapes my lips and I immediately regret it.

I suck in some air and pray that I have the energy to deal with her on top of everything else. "Okay, so I want you to think about what you want to say.

I mean, of course you can say that she is a good girl and things like that, but you also need to say something personal."

"Like what?"

"I don't know, something that humanizes her." Damn it, there's that word again. I bite my tongue. "Something that just makes people want to root for her."

"I have no idea what you're talking about," Mom says.

"Okay." I shift my weight from one foot to another, trying to think of something. "You can say how much she loved animals and how she had all of these friends at school."

"She didn't though," Mom says.

"She didn't?"

"No."

"What are you talking about? This is news to me."

"Well, I mean, she knew people at school, but she was always taking pictures of them for the yearbook and different projects, and I don't think many of them liked that."

I hesitate for a moment and my thoughts return back to that video that Captain Talarico showed me.

She was in the room and she was recording Natalie and Neil having sex on the couch. What was she doing there? From the way that the video was shot, it was clear that they knew that she was present, but why?

I haven't had the chance to talk to either of them about it yet. Neil's parents have basically kicked me off their property and told me to only go through their lawyer.

Natalie's a whole other story.

"I'm going to go to the station and try to find out what happened with Natalie. We'll be having the press conference there. Do you know where it's located?"

"Yeah, right by the courthouse?"

"Yes, exactly. Anyway, I think I'm going to go there around seven thirty to see what I can find out, but you need to be there at eight thirty at the latest and try to think of something human."

"Human, I got it," Mom says, enunciating the word.

To my annoyance, Mom returns to her book without saying another word and I stand in the doorway like an idiot waiting to say something else.

Luckily, my phone goes off in my back pocket and after I look at the screen, I have to take the call.

"Hi, Captain Medvil," I say.

"Yeah, I meant to call you earlier. I need an update on the Kaslar situation," he says.

"I thought that Lenore was going to give you the gist."

"Yeah, he did, but he's an officer and you're a detective the last time I checked." Captain Medvil is clearly peeved.

I swallow hard, walk past Sydney, and out onto the porch. I need some privacy for this. I can't whisper. I have to talk in my normal tone of voice, but I definitely can't do that in this small house if I don't want my mom and Sydney to hear me getting yelled at.

As soon as I step outside, I regret the decision immediately. A cold gust of wind swirls around me and I'm wearing nothing but a thin long sleeve shirt that's cropped a little bit too short.

I tuck what I can of the shirt into the waistband of my jeans, but that only keeps some of the cold away. Flurries are already starting to fall and the temperature must be in the mid-thirties at the most.

"I'm going to submit my report very soon. By tonight."

"I heard that you went back to Big Bear. Any news with your sister?"

"No, but there's a press conference tomorrow morning, so I wanted to be here. There's actually another girl who has gone missing, her friend, under very similar circumstances, so it doesn't look good," I say.

"Okay, sorry to hear that," he says in his most professional tone.

I nod and bite my lower lip but say nothing.

"Kaslar, what's new? What update do you have?" he barks.

He doesn't have the best cell phone etiquette or in-person etiquette for that matter. Even his emails are clipped and often contain one or two words formed into a sentence.

"I interviewed him. His wife is missing. Last time he saw her was before her business trip three ago."

"Do you have the details or not?"

"Not with me, sir, but you'll have them all in the report," I repeat myself without outwardly saying that I had already mentioned the report and annoying him further.

"What was your sense from him?"

"He was very shady and shifty. He kept putting his hood up and down, avoiding eye contact."

"So, a suspect?"

"I have to talk to her friend, Elin. She's the one that pushed him to make the report. She was the one who dropped her off after the business trip and then she disappeared. His wife had an appointment to go to the gynecologist, and she didn't show up. I have to confirm that still. She also stood her friend up for lunch as well. So, it's all a little bit confusing as to what could have happened."

"Well, the husband could have done it, right?"

"In this case it's a possibility or she might've just disappeared, I don't know. I mean, if she thinks that she's pregnant and she doesn't have a good relationship with her husband. Apparently, he was not very supportive of her selling these candles for this networking company that she works for. I still have to talk to her boss, find out if maybe there were some financial problems that she was encountering. There's a lot more interviewing to take place."

"Yeah, I'm glad to hear you say that, Carr," he says.

"I'm sorry, I know that I'm on this case, but is there any way I could take tomorrow off? Personal day. I really need to be here for the press conference."

"Yeah, I understand. How about this? Come back tomorrow afternoon, right after the conference. It's at nine, right?"

"Yeah," I nod, "they typically are."

"Okay, well, be there, do the interview, and help out as much as you can, but I expect you back here in the afternoon if you want to keep working on this case."

I exhale suddenly.

"Kaitlyn," he says, rarely using my first name.

"Yeah?" I perk up.

"I can easily take you off the Kaslar case if it's too much. You can stay there, take a week, and try to find your sister."

"I don't know." I hesitate.

"You have to consider that."

I think about it.

The tone of his voice is suddenly soft and it puts me into an uncomfortable situation. It doesn't sound like him.

"If you make that decision, then you're going to have to know that you're going to go to the back of the line in terms of catching new cases. I can only do this once. Next time something happens, there's a murder to investigate, you're on it. No more days."

"Yeah, that's not going to work, Captain," I say with a heavy sigh. "I don't know if I'll be able to help or do anything while I'm here in the next few days and I need to save my personal time."

"That's what I thought you'd say. Good. Okay, so just drive back tomorrow afternoon and I expect you to interview Elin, her boss, the doctor, and all the people who might know about her whereabouts. I expect to see a report tomorrow night."

"Okay, yeah."

"It's not going to be a problem, right?" he asks.

"No, no, not at all," I promise.

I hang up the phone, put it on the rail, and look out at the neighbor's falling down fence. They haven't lived here in years and use it primarily as a second home to capitalize on the thriving ski market in the winters. As a result, it has fallen into a lot of disrepair, but the people that rent it for the weekends don't really care. The owners, who now live in San Diego, don't either. The only ones who are left with the eyesore are us, or rather, my mom. I wrap my hands around my shoulders, not wanting to go back inside.

Another strong gust of wind blows through and tosses my hair into my face. I tuck a few strands behind my ears and feel completely out of control. I know that I should stay here longer and look for my sister, but I also need to go back and do my job. If I give up this case, then who knows what kind of case I'll get assigned to next. With my luck, it will probably be a lot more urgent.

So far, I don't know if Mrs. Kaslar or rather Ms. Moore, since she goes by her maiden name, has disappeared of her own volition. She might have. I just have to do a few interviews and then get back up here. She might even show up and close this whole thing altogether, but if I catch a murder case, then that's forty-eight hours of nonstop work to try to solve it. I'm sure you know that most cases are solved within forty-eight hours and the others, well, they become a little bit more complicated.

Anyway, my best bet is to do what I told him I would. Stay here, go to the press conference, try to stay there for the beginning of the search, and hope that I can split my time between my two worlds. One thing that I haven't talked to my mom about, or with the sheriff's department here about at all is a search party. We need to organize that as soon as possible.

Typically, it's done in liaison with the law enforcement agency overseeing the investigation, in this case, the sheriff's station, but I haven't heard anyone there mention it before.

I suck in some air and open the front door. I find Sydney sitting in the recliner looking at Violet's yearbook pictures. In one she's sitting in the commons in the middle school, eating lunch with that innocent grin on her face and AirPods shoved in her ears.

"That was Captain Medvil," I say. "I have to go back and do these interviews about this possible missing persons case that I'm on, but I don't have to be back until tomorrow afternoon, so I wanted to ask, would you help me organize a search party?"

"Yes, of course. When?" she asks as if almost an afterthought.

"We have to start tonight. I don't have much time."

"Yes, of course."

8

Sydney and I work well into the night. My mom goes to bed around nine, but we stay up until at least two. I've never organized a search party by myself before, but I've seen it done. We put out a call and we make posters. We lay out the poster in Canva.com since neither of us are too familiar with Photoshop and we post them on various social media platforms and Facebook groups.

The basics of organizing a search for a missing person are not very complicated. What's complicated, and harder, is to get enough people involved so that you're able to cover a big enough area.

Police will usually only conduct searches if they believe that someone's disappearance is suspicious.

That tends to be the case for Violet. I want to put together a plan to start the process as soon as possible. Typically, when a person goes missing, you have to ask permission from the landowner before searching anyone's property.

The last time that Violet was seen was right here on this property and I have already conducted a pretty close search of about a mile radius from here. Ideally when the volunteers show up, you have a record of names and contact details of every single person prior to embarking on the search.

Typically volunteers under eighteen are excluded because people may be found in all sorts of conditions, dead, or alive. What about in this case? What if some of her friends want to help out? I'm not sure.

I've participated in a few search operations and it's best to separate people into small teams of eight to twelve people per area, making sure that everyone there knows not to touch anything that could be potential evidence and instead, take a photo of anything that they might think is of significance.

This all depends on how many people show up to volunteer in the first place. I find a grid of the area online, print it out, and mark it up into grids.

Each person in charge of a specific area would be the map holder and that will be the person who will assign people to different areas on the grid.

The group of eight to twelve people will then be broken down into even smaller groups, if possible, and spread out into the various grids to make sure that every single place is searched thoroughly. If anyone comes across anything suspicious, that area is tagged with a piece of bright colored tape and the police are called, if they haven't already been. Naturally, all cliffs, trees, and ditches have to be checked as well.

Sydney has never participated in a search and I go over these details with her.

"What about video cameras?" she asks.

"I checked with the neighbors around here and there was only one camera that was on at the time and there wasn't anything suspicious on it at all. Two others were disconnected. Of course, the sheriff's department is reviewing that stuff at the moment. I guess we'll just have to see."

"How many people do you think we can get to do the search?"

"I don't know," I say. She shakes her head.

"There's a little bit of activity on these groups that you told me to join and post on, but so far it's all crickets."

"Well, maybe we'll have better luck overnight. I don't know. In any case, let's get some rest. It's almost two in the morning," I say, looking at the time. "I think we've done a lot. We have the invitations, the flyers, and things like that. Let's try to get this search going by ten o'clock. No, by eleven o'clock. Maybe we can have some people volunteer right from the press conference."

"That's not a lot of time."

"I know, but I have to get back to work for later. Theoretically, my mom can continue running it or maybe somebody from the department."

"Do you still not know how her friend, Natalie, is connected to this?"

"No, I don't even know if her disappearance is connected. In fact, I don't really know much about her disappearance at all. Let's just get some rest," I say.

She follows me to my old bedroom. I have a queen-size bed and we share. When she gets under the covers, I turn off the light and fall asleep quickly, but restlessly.

THE FOLLOWING MORNING, I wake up early. It's barely six. I'm usually a deep sleeper who needs hours of rest, but the four hours that I've gotten hasn't really relaxed me anymore than I was last night.

I'm wide awake without any caffeine. I tiptoe past my mom's room into the living room as I go to make myself some hot tea, mint, to take the chill off. The house is never very warm. Back in LA, in my apartment, I have poor insulation and single pane windows. I always pay through the nose for heating, but I keep my place warm and a comfortable seventy-four degrees. I can wear a t-shirt if I want to, but most of the time I wear long sleeves.

That's probably a reaction to having grown up here. It's not that it's just cold outside. It's that my mom runs warm and she doesn't like spending money on heating. So, I grew up always wearing three sweaters and lots of layers nine months out of the year. I promised myself when I went to college that no matter my financial situation, I'd never wear gloves inside while doing homework again. No more sixty-five-degree evenings for me and I've pretty much kept that promise ever since then.

My phone rings and I'm surprised that anyone outside of work would be contacting me at this hour. When I look at the screen, I see that it's Luke.

I hesitate. I don't want to answer. I can't remember how many days it has been since we've spoken, but it has been enough for me to get annoyed.

Finally, I pick up the phone.

"Why are you calling me?" I ask.

"What do you mean? I wanted to see how you are and what's been going on."

"I thought that you were ignoring me."

"No, I am out here on the job. Sacramento. Remember?"

"Yeah, but you said that you would be in touch."

"Well, I'm sorry I couldn't get back to you earlier. We were doing some undercover work and then some trainings. You know how it is."

"Yeah. I guess."

"What's wrong? Are you mad?"

I hesitate.

"Oh, shit. I just realized what time it is. Sorry. I'm really wired from being up all night on a stakeout."

I nod.

"I'd tell you more, but you know, I don't really want to go into it right now. Can't really go into it right now."

"Yeah, sure. Of course. Whatever," I say.

"Listen, I'm going to be back maybe Friday. Can we grab dinner?"

I try to think back to what day of the week it is.

"I'm in Big Bear now about to do a press conference about my sister."

"Yes, of course. How is that? Any news?"

"Actually, her friend is missing now, too. She disappeared after she got dropped off. She never came home. No one knows where she is."

"That's unbelievable," Luke says. I hear the creaking of his chair as he sits back. "Really?"

"Yeah. I don't know. I have no idea if it's related or not. I drove up here last night. I haven't met up with the sheriff yet."

"How long are you staying?"

"I have to be back to do some interviews for a case back in LA, so not that long, but I hope that I can at least get the search party going before I leave."

"Okay. Let me know if you need anything or if there's anything I can do to help."

"Yeah, sure."

"Hey," he says after a long pause, "are you okay?"

"Yeah. I'm just surprised that you called…at all."

"No, listen, I was not ghosting you. I was just out for work, you know how it is."

"Yeah, I do," I say, even though I also know that text messages are able to be sent on stakeouts, especially when you have hours of time just sitting in the car, waiting around for something to happen. Of course, I don't say any of this.

"So, can I see you on Friday?"

"Maybe," I say, trying to be as casual as possible. "If I'm back home and I'm not too tired, maybe."

"Okay, good because I'd really like to. I had a good time, Carr."

I laugh. I like that. A lot of people in this business tend to call you by your last name, but it sounds different coming out of his mouth.

"Listen, my mom's getting up. I have to go get ready."

"Okay. Good luck. Let me know how it goes," he says and hangs up.

I smile looking at my phone. That was unexpected and kind of welcoming.

"Who was that?" Mom asks, starting the coffee.

I look around and look at her. A small smile forms on my face.

"A boy?" she asks, winking at me mischievously.

"Yeah, maybe," I mumble.

"You don't have to hide these things from me, Kaitlyn. I'm your mother. I want you to be happy."

"I know," I say.

"Was that the FBI agent?"

"Yes. Apparently, he didn't call because he got stuck at work."

"Good. Well, if anyone were to understand that it would be you, right?"

"Yeah," I mumble with a shrug.

Sydney and I arrive at the sheriff's station around seven forty-five, a good hour before the press conference. My mom stays home and promises to get there by eight thirty.

I debated for a while as to what exactly to wear to this meeting because this isn't just having a conversation with a bunch of cops. I have to look appropriate, feminine, and reverential as the sister of the missing girl.

I of all people know how difficult it is to get the press interested in the story. My mom doesn't. She thinks that every missing girl that she sees on the news is all that there is, but that's not true. The girls that tend to make it on the news are the ones that are cute, pretty, blonde, and white. There are some girls of all races, and all complexions, with all hair colors, that go missing every day, but they don't sell well.

If they don't make the public care about them in picture form, no one is going to report on them. They might make a statement, throw a picture when the news is kind of light and there isn't much else going on in the world, but you're not going to get the kind of 24/7 news coverage that Laci Peterson or Natalee Holloway got back in the day.

In order to get that kind of recognition, you need all the pieces of the puzzle to be just right; attractive victim, suspicious circumstances, and a beautiful family. It usually helps if you're well off as well.

We don't tick a lot of these boxes. My mom is a single mom. My dad was a low-level drug dealer with a record. What helps is that we do live in a small town and people like small town stories. What also helps is that Violet is thirteen and there are some cute pictures of her. She's an innocent victim and I hope that story leads the evening news, at least on some of the channels in Southern California.

I show up at the station in a delicate maroon blouse that will probably look good on television. It's not something I usually wear, but everything needs to be just perfect in order for this press conference to become a news story.

Sydney wears her typical work attire; suit jacket, suit pants, heels. Her hair is pulled up in a nice bun, but mine isn't. I don't want to fret with anything, my hair or makeup, when I'm getting ready to go on camera. So, I do it all before I even get here.

"You look good," Sydney whispers.

As we walk into the station, I feel extremely overdressed, but that's part of the game.

———————

THE SHERIFF'S station has low ceilings and poor lighting made up of fluorescents that don't do anyone any favors. I wave hello to the desk deputy upfront and show our identification. He points me in the direction of Captain Talarico's office.

I've been there already, but I haven't met this deputy, so, I let him give us the tour. The bathrooms are on the right in the center of the room, kind of in a public place, but oh well. The captain's office is in the far corner. The only place with a little bit of privacy.

I knock and introduce Sydney. He waves us both in and continues to type something on the computer. He's in his fifties and the lines on his face are pretty well-ingrained, permanent, and not going anywhere. He has fine hair and a standard issue crew cut with big jowls but surprisingly, striking cheekbones.

There's a big plastic container with a 7-Eleven logo on it. He takes sips of his ice-cold soda from it occasionally, as he speaks.

"So, you're a detective as well?" Captain Talarico asks Sydney.

"Yeah. Homicide, LA."

"Wow. We got a lot of attractive detectives out in the LAPD now, huh?"

"Well, you know, they did start hiring more women so the attractiveness level can only go up, right?" Sydney jokes back. She has always been the one who could take the sexist jokes.

Personally, I wish I could have the same approach, but after years of this, I get really tired of comments about my looks and my makeup, which are basically statements about how I'm probably not as good at my job as a man would be.

Not a lot of people know this, but a detective's job is to ask questions, to get people to open up to you, and to admit mistakes on television. We do some running around, chasing down criminals, and that sort of thing, but most of the time our job is to get people to confess.

This isn't a strenuous position, unless you are talking about just the sheer number of hours that you have to put in. Frankly, if we're going to be making blanket generalizations, that doesn't mean very much.

I wait for Captain Talarico to say something else, but luckily, he doesn't.

I don't have to tell him that we are not here in any official capacity. He knows that we're way out of our jurisdiction. So, I bite my tongue when the thought crosses my mind.

"Any news or anything else since last time we spoke?" I ask.

"Nope, unfortunately not. I had my deputies check a bunch of Nest cameras and recordings from the neighbors up and down the street, even around the corner. Everybody's been putting those up since we've been spotting black bears in the area, you know?"

"Yeah, that's good," I say.

"No luck. There was no recording of her getting dropped off or her getting into any car."

"Wait. So, you think that Nancy Dillinger is lying? She didn't actually drop her off?"

"Didn't say that. There's actually no camera that points directly at your house at the spot where she said she had dropped her off. Unfortunately," he says, licking the tip of his pen and looking through some more paperwork in the folder with my sister's name on top.

That is the first time I've ever seen her name in this way, now missing officially. Even though she has been missing for a few days, this makes it real.

The folder with her name on it is crinkled, used, licked. The sticker reads 'Violet Carr.' If we don't find her soon, this folder's going to grow to two, three, four, perhaps even a whole box.

That would mean that she's either missing forever or likely dead.

My mind starts to feel muddled so I exhale quickly.

"We worked on organizing a search," I say.

"Without us?"

"It was last night when we got in, and I don't have much time. I have to go back to work. This is what we came up with." I pull out my phone and show him the pamphlet inviting people to the search party. "Who knows, maybe the guy who did this is going to show up and participate. Weirder things have happened."

"You should not have done this without my authorization."

"I didn't want to call you at ten in the evening while you were at home."

"Why? Do you stop working at ten?" he asks, tilting his head in my direction. "I don't. Not when I have a little girl missing."

"I'm sorry. I just wanted to do something last night. We posted this on a few Facebook groups and I got the map together. I made the grids. If we get enough volunteers, then we can check all of these places. I mean, of course I've already made my way around this grid a number of times, but it's good to have an official search party."

"Of course it is. That's why usually these things are done working with the police."

"I'm sorry, okay?" I apologize again. I'm not sure what else I can do.

"Don't do it again," he snaps and then tells me to send my pamphlet over to him to print out.

"I wanted to have this all organized for the news broadcast. I'm hoping maybe someone will join right after the press conference."

"Well, none of that stuff is going to air until noon tomorrow. So, if you want to use a press conference to spread the word, the earliest this thing can happen is in the afternoon."

I hesitate.

"You have a problem with that?"

"I have to go back to LA. I have a case."

"Well, we can always do one this afternoon and another one tomorrow morning. That will give people more time to get involved. You do realize you're going to need at least twenty or thirty people for this to be any sort of search party?"

"Yeah," I say.

"You do realize that it gets dark early now, and it's best to do it during the day."

"Yes, of course." He's lecturing me as if I'm a child, as if I have no idea what I'm talking about. I hate it, but there's nothing I can do about it. I need his help.

"Okay. I'll get my deputies involved, assign someone to this job. Let's say three o'clock today and then noon tomorrow. Would that give you enough time to get back?"

"Yes. Yes, it will." I nod, even though I have no idea if I'm actually telling the truth. "Can I ask you about Natalie?" I ask when he nods toward the door for us to leave.

"Natalie is missing as well," he says, shaking his head. "It's unclear what happened, same as your sister."

"Did someone drop her off?"

"Yeah. Her boyfriend Neil said that he dropped her off at nine p.m. We're going through the video cameras now. We should have a better view of what happened because a lot of people in that neighborhood have cameras set up, a lot more than in yours, and there are fewer trees and obstructions in the way. So, if at least a few of them are working, we should be able to tell if he's telling the truth."

"When are you going to find out?"

"We have deputies going to the houses as we speak. This just happened last night. So she didn't come back all night. Her mom was distraught, naturally."

"Do you think the cases are connected?" I ask.

"I don't know. It seems like a really odd coincidence, otherwise. Two girls, the same school who know each other, and who were acquaintances."

"I'm not a big believer in coincidences," Sydney says and I immediately wish that she hadn't.

"Me neither."

Captain Talarico laughs, clearly taking it as a joke.

"Are there cops who believe in coincidences? If anything, we're more of a conspiracy theory set, right?" He grabs his Big Gulp and sucks down a few mouthfuls of soda.

We have a few minutes before the press conference. Sydney and I walk out to get some coffee and maybe breakfast. The vending machine doesn't offer much in terms of selection, but I still stand here staring at the options, trying to decide whether eight forty-five in the morning is an okay time to have a chocolate bar.

Maybe it is.

Maybe when your sister goes missing and then so does her friend.

Maybe all bets are off at that point.

9

"You're going to be fine," Sydney says, rubbing in between my shoulder blades.

I take a few heavy breaths in and let them out very slowly, trying to find that calming breath that my yoga teacher's always talking about. Damn it, I should've gone there more often. There's no way you can get rid of all of this tension after just a few sessions.

"I just need to get through this," I say, pressing A3 for the pack of M&M's. Sydney buys me a small cup of coffee and dumps a bunch of cream into it, which I hate, but I don't bother telling her this. I take a few swigs and then pop a handful of M&M's into my mouth to make the taste go away.

I told Sydney about the videos last night. I had her promise not to tell my mom, but I had to tell someone. Violet and Natalie are involved in something. The cops know this, of course.

Are they gone because of those videos that she made? Is that the reason? They're keeping that under wraps. No one would care about a girl like her if the news people let all of that get out. No, she has to look innocent and unmarred in order for this to make the news.

Mom comes in about ten minutes before the start of the news conference looking terrible. Her hair is disheveled. Her makeup looks like it has been put on and then removed with some sort of abrasive substance. Even her top and her skirt are mismatched.

"Mom, what's going on? Why do you... Why are you like this?"

"I don't know. I just couldn't handle it. I was crying so much. I can't talk to them. I don't know what you mean by making her look human. I'm just so distraught."

My jaw clenches up, distraught is an odd word to use for someone who is actually distraught. That's a descriptive noun, not a word that someone who is lost and actually distraught uses.

"Mom, you're going to do this interview. You have to. You're her mother."

"No, I can't. I can't. I've been watching those interviews of the parents of the missing children and they always look so put together, so perfect. I'm just not like that. You know that I don't really speak well in public."

"Like I do?" I hiss at her.

"What are you even talking about?"

This isn't the right time to remind her of the fact that I once threw up because I had to do a presentation in tenth grade or the fact that I froze on stage when she forced me to participate in some pageant in elementary school. If I have to go there, I will.

"Listen, I know that you have problems, but you make these sorts of speeches all the time," Mom says. "I mean, I saw you on the news. Reading off a piece of paper reporting what you found."

"This is my sister."

"Exactly. This is why you will be so much better at it," Mom says. "I mean, look at me. I can't go up there like this. I look like a homeless person."

One side of her hair is pressed tightly against her head, but the other looks like it has been brushed out and now it's frizzy as a result. She's not wearing even a little bit of foundation, making all her age spots and the oily parts of her face completely visible. If she were to go on camera right now, no one would care. There's a fine line between looking like you're grieving and looking like you have lost it completely.

Sydney pulls me aside.

"You can't let her do this," she says, as if I don't know this already. "She's going to blow this and they're not going to report on your sister. You have to do it."

"Oh my God," I say. It comes out more like a growl of desperation. "I'm not even here. I don't even live here."

"It doesn't matter. People have a family member who usually speaks and everyone else just stands there. That's what you have to do."

"I have some makeup with me. I can clean her up and put a jacket on her to cover that atrocious blouse."

"You can't trust her to do the talking, okay? Please?"

I give her a nod. I know that everything she's saying is true, but I also know that I don't want all of this pressure laying on my shoulders. Then again, who else would take care of it?

Hasn't it always been this way?

Mom being too distraught and overwhelmed by her feelings to deal with anything. I have always been the one who filled in the holes, who made sure that the family was fine.

After my father's death, my mom was a wreck, as you can imagine. She was so much of a wreck that she didn't even stop me from finding his body; and then she was too upset to say anything at the funeral. She didn't care that I was terrified of speaking in public. On top of that, I didn't even know anything good to say.

I didn't know what to say in an eulogy. I didn't know how to make my father, who I was desperately angry with, sound like a decent person after all of the years of awfulness that he had put me through. She didn't care though. She said she just couldn't do it and that was it.

Right now, it's the same thing all over again. Yes, it's her daughter who's missing and she's my sister, but Mom has been utterly helpless since the beginning of this debacle.

So, why would she be any different now?

I go to the bathroom, check my makeup, use the toilet, and reapply my lipstick.

I walk out with a stony expression on my face. As soon as I greet the reporters and get behind the podium, I soften it to look pleasant, beautiful, and welcoming. It's an overt decision. I can feel my lips relaxing. I let my eyelids rest a little bit, despite the fact that there are blinding lights in my face.

I look at the camera. I plead. I pretend that there's one person on the other end who's holding her hostage and I plead for him to let Violet go.

"Please, whatever you want, just tell us, with no questions asked. We need her. I need my sister back. She's just thirteen years old. If you know anything about her or her whereabouts, you have to come forward. Please." This is my part of the job, to be the family, to be the one in grief, in a public manner so that people believe us.

The other part of the job belongs to the captain and the director of communications from the sheriff's department who had previously gone over the details about her disappearance. It was a conscious decision not to bring up her disappearance in conjunction with Natalie's quite yet, since it just happened, and the deputies weren't able to go through all of the cameras and interview all of the neighbors.

The last thing the sheriff's department wants is for Natalie to show back up after just sleeping over at a friend's house and have all of the reporters forget about Violet as a result, assuming that she would come back, too.

"You did a good job," Captain Talarico says after the lights go off and we walk out into the hallway.

"Yeah?"

"Yeah. You really sold it."

"Well, wasn't so much of an act."

"Yeah, but it takes a lot of practice. Not everyone can do it."

I nod. I know what he means. Some people appear aloof on camera. They clench up. They don't want to talk. If there's ever a camera thrown into your face, you have to lean in. You have to participate. You have to engage. You have to make the people on the other side of it believe that you're telling the truth.

Out of the corner of my eye I see a reporter with KTLA walking out, draping her bag over her shoulder. I pull myself away from the captain and approach her.

"Hi, I'm sorry, Miranda. I'm sorry to bother you. I just wanted to thank you for coming and helping me to find my sister."

"Yes, of course," she says kind of casually, not really engaging.

Unlike her on-air personality, she seems to be distracted, probably worried about the next job and the next place that she needs to go to.

"Can I give you my card?" I ask. "Please? Call me anytime, day or night, in case you get any leads."

She looks down and reads my job title. Suddenly her interest is piqued.

"You're a detective?"

"Yes, homicide."

"Oh. Did you say that?"

"Yeah, I mentioned it on air, but-"

"Oh, wow. Okay. I must've missed that. I guess it was when you introduced yourself, but you're actually a homicide detective and your sister is missing."

"Yeah." I nod. "Why is that relevant?"

"Well, it's unusual, for one. Would you mind doing a one-on-one interview with me?"

"Not at all," I say.

WE FIND an empty room and her cameraman comes over and sets up. The bright lights come back on and I don't have anything in which to check my makeup or attire, except for my phone.

I have two sweat stains underneath my arms growing bigger with every passing minute, but I hope to God that if I press my arms close to my sides, they won't be too visible.

"I'm not sure how much of this we can air, but I would just love to hear anything that you can tell me about your sister."

I tell her the whole story again, mentioning a few more details like how sweet and loving she is, straight A student, never sneaks out at night, and never had a boyfriend.

"She wasn't anything like me when I was a kid," I add.

"Well, you turned out pretty good, Detective Carr."

"Yeah. There was that iffy time in high school where I could have really gone either way," I joke.

She asks me a few more questions and I answer, nothing unusual, just more details about Violet growing up, my parents, and that kind of thing.

At the end, I gloss over the details and emphasize the small town and my life now in LA. She seems to like the quaint angle in place. I know that she's not really wishing for my sister to be dead, but all reporters wish for some sort of resolution just so you have more of a story to report on.

"I'm not sure how much of this will air. It will really depend on my boss," Miranda says, shaking my hand at the end. Her nails are perfect, immaculate, just like her contouring and her hair. There's no team traveling with her so I know that she does it all herself.

She looks so good, she could be a YouTube beauty influencer.

"I appreciate anything you can do. I just really want to get the word out as much as possible."

"Yes, of course. Again, I'm really sorry." She gives me her card and tells me goodbye.

10

Later that morning, I watch the press conference on television with my mom and Sydney, which we switched around between channels, but they all show the same thing. At the end, they announced what time the volunteers are needed to participate in the search effort, along with the meeting place.

I take the video of the broadcast from KTLA and share it on the newly created Find Violet Carr Facebook and Instagram pages that we have just set up.

"What about TikTok?" Sydney asks.

"What about it?"

"Well, a lot of older people are on Facebook, but you won't find any little kids on there anymore.

I've had a case be solved with the help of the kids on TikTok. Why not make an account there as well?"

"Yeah, sure," I say, realizing that I've never used the site before.

I download the app when I have a free second and take a look around. I've heard about it. It's popular with people who like to dance and make funny little videos of themselves. I know that it'll take me a little bit to figure out how to use it and how to tag it properly so it gets out to the right people.

"You think her friends are on it?" I ask Sydney.

"Pretty sure."

"I should probably search for their names just in case."

"Yeah, of course." Sydney nods.

Mom has very little interest in this. She has a Facebook account, but she rarely uses it, except to stay in touch with her friends. I show her the page and how to share it. She's the local here and I wonder how many more people will open up to her rather than me about my sister.

"Mom, are you listening?" I ask, showing her the page again. "I'm going to leave. I have to go back to work tonight. So, I want you to be here and check it, see if anyone writes anything."

"Yeah. Sure, of course," she says rather absentmindedly.

"Mom, you really have to pay attention. I need your help."

"I'm here, aren't I?" she asks as if being here is an imposition.

"What happened? What's wrong?" I press.

"I don't know, nothing. I just didn't get very much sleep last night."

"Yeah, I know," I say, noting silently that she actually went to bed around nine.

I went to bed at two, but hey, who's comparing, right?

"You are going to be there at the search party, right? I can't."

"Why can't you come?" she asks, folding her hands.

"Mom. I already did everything, okay? I mean, I set it up. I just can't be there today. I have to get back. I have a case I'm working on."

"Don't you think that your sister's disappearance is more important?"

"Mom, if I take another day off, or another couple of days, there's no guarantee that Violet will be back, but there is a guarantee that I'm going to be assigned to some murder case that will have a dead body and all sorts of leads, which would put me in LA for a good week. I won't be able to come back, okay? That's what I'm trying to avoid."

"Yeah, I get it," she says, waving her hand though I can tell that she's upset. Tired of the back and forth, I decide to leave.

I tell her goodbye and give her the location where the search party is going to be meeting up. They're setting up not too far away from her house. I tell her to be there right at three p.m.

I'm leaving a little bit earlier than I thought that I would, but I've had enough. Besides, if I can avoid some of the LA traffic, I can get back to the city, do my interviews, and hopefully gain some traction on this Moore Kaslar case.

THE DRIVE back to LA is rather uneventful. Sydney and I talk about Violet a little bit and then about Luke.

After I drop her off, I try to put all of my personal issues out of my mind so that I can focus entirely on the Karen Moore Kaslar disappearance. After Elin texts the address, I'm surprised when my GPS takes me to Park La Brea apartments. This is the place where Mark lived when we dated and where I had spent almost every day and night of our relationship. My apartment, closer to campus, was used more like a crashing pad where I took occasional naps in between classes.

I think back to that time and how utterly devoted we were to one another. I guess some people might call it toxic, but we just wanted to spend every waking minute together and nothing was going to stop us. I drive through the familiar gate as Elin beeps me in and I park in the visitor parking lot just like I used to, back in the day.

There are towers looking over West LA, each with thirteen floors. Mark lived on the twelfth floor. He had a huge floor-to-ceiling window looking out onto the green fields below. All the apartments are set up around a park with playgrounds and workout equipment.

They're almost like their own little town with larger townhouses, offering more luxury to the side closest to The Grove, and more city-like. This is where people with families typically live. On the other side of the park stands the towers with gorgeous views of the Hollywood Hills. This is where we lived, or rather Mark and his roommate.

They had a two bedroom with an enormous living room that was unlike any other two bedroom I've ever lived in since. Elin lives in one of the lower apartments facing a playground. I press the button to her apartment and she buzzes me in. The floors and the walls look completely different, but then again, it was years ago when I was here.

Elin is a heavy-set woman who looks to be about my age with big eyes and long hair that has a few extensions sticking out just a little bit. There are pictures of her and her friends all over her hallway. I can tell that, under normal circumstances, she looks a lot better. She's dressed in camouflage-colored leggings, bare feet, and a gray tank top with a sports bra underneath.

She welcomes me inside and her little yappy dog jumps up on my ankles and barks loudly. I kneel down to pet her after asking if it's okay. After a few minutes, the dog and I are friends. Pepper makes herself comfortable in my lap and demands pets.

"Thanks for making the time to see me," I say.

"No, thank you for coming by. I'm just really worried about where she could be. It's been another whole day."

Elin looks nervous and distressed.

"Can you tell me what happened? Can you tell me more about your relationship? More about yourself?"

"Yeah, sure," Elin says, twirling her finger around her hair.

She slides around on her leather couch. It's white, soft, and covered in fluffy throw pillows, like the kind you see in Bed Bath & Beyond catalogs college edition.

"I don't know where to start," she says again while sitting down, tucking her hands underneath her thighs and leaning close to me.

I pull out my recorder and put it down in front of her.

"Would you mind if I record this conversation?"

"No. No, not at all."

"Okay. Thanks," I say and repeat myself once the recorder is going. She agrees one more time. Then I dive right in. "Can you tell me about yourself and how do you know Karen Moore Kaslar?"

"Well, we met at a Jamba Juice and then we realized we were in the same yoga class. It was at the YMCA on the corner. I had never been there before and neither had she, but we didn't want to pay much. I guess we independently saw that they were having these classes for only ten dollars each. We signed up because the other ones up for like twenty or twenty-five bucks and that's just too much. We started talking and decided to go to coffee. We became friends. She doesn't live very far from here, so we could always meet at The Grove and get some brunch, that kind of thing. Her husband works a lot."

"Yeah. Do you know Robert?"

"Yeah. But I don't want to say anything bad."

"Please. You have to be as honest with me as possible. Your friend is missing and I'm trying to help you find her."

"I don't know what to say. I met him once. First time she invited me over to watch a movie and have some wine. It was fine. I mean, he seemed friendly enough. He was just sort of walking by. I kept inviting him out with us to a bar or something like that, but he never wanted to come. He said he was too tired from work. That was when he was still working on his PhD."

"Okay. Yeah. What about you? Do you live here alone?"

"No," she says. "My husband lives here, too. It's a two bedroom."

"Oh, okay. Sorry. I just saw the door to the one room," I say, actually surprised.

"Yeah, we have a child and we're trying to have another one. So, we're not going to be staying here for long."

"Okay. How old is your child?"

"Nine months. It was great. We're working on buying a house, but LA prices and all."

"Are they somewhere together now?"

"Yeah. I just wanted to talk to you without interruptions. So he took her to the park that's just right downstairs. That's probably the one thing I'm going to miss about this place."

"Yeah, I get it," I say. I've given stuff like that practically no thought. "So, you two hit it off, right?"

"Yeah, we did. We've been friends for about half a year or so."

"You're also business partners?" I lead her.

"Well, yeah. I mean, not partners, but I told her about how I was making money. I'm selling candles for Candle Love. Maybe you've heard of it?"

I shake my head.

"It's a network marketing company. We're all each on our own. We're all entrepreneurs."

"Her husband mentioned how she had to buy all of these supplies in order to sell them first."

"Well, yes." I feel her getting agitated. She twists her hair around and pulls her hands from underneath her butt and places them firmly on her knees. "Of course he would say something like that. Robert, he just has no patience for anything like that. He just doesn't believe that she can be successful."

"Can you tell me what you mean by that?"

"Well, in Candle Love, we all know how important it is to be engaged with your business and have a supportive partner who will believe that you can become successful. What can you do? I mean, he wasn't like that. He thought it was a big scam. You have to invest in your business. If you were going to start a bookstore, a coffee shop, or any other business, you'd have to buy supplies and you'd have to spend money marketing, that kind of thing. This one had very little costs up front. Yet he still complained about it."

"He told me that it was $4,000 in candles?"

"It wasn't just candles. There were gift packages and gift boxes. That kind of thing. You don't just sell candles, you sell a scent experience."

"Oh, okay. I got it," I say.

Suddenly, she shifts into selling mode. She goes over to the console table, opens the drawers, and pulls out different types of candles packaged in a variety of different ways.

One smells like peach, another like ginger. In addition to the candle, there's also the box and the presentation of it all. One is packaged elegantly into a glass container while the other lays on a box of wooden splinters, which I'm about to point out is probably not the safest thing, but it does look nice.

She shows me all the various boxes and packages, moving her hand around in an elegant sort of way like they do on the Home Shopping Network.

I quickly try to shift the conversation back to Karen.

"So, tell me what happened. You went on a business trip with her?"

"Yes." She puts the box down on the coffee table and looks directly at me. "We went on a business trip. It was a conference, basically showing us how to be better entrepreneurs. It was really inspiring. They had all of these business leaders there and motivational speakers. We just knew that this was going to happen. This was finally going to work out for us."

"Finally?"

"Well, I'm having struggles as much as she is. After the initial few sales, it's hard. People have such a negative view of network marketing nowadays. It's like, anytime you reach out to one of your old friends from high school, they just shut you down."

"Oh, I understand. So, you went through basic? So, what are you doing? What were you told to do? How is Karen getting sales now?"

"I think she sold about $1,000 worth of candles initially when she first joined. Of course, Robert was very happy about it, but then things sort of dried up like they tend to, unless you recruit more of your own people into your network to join the organization and become entrepreneurs themselves. Not everyone has it in them to run their own company. Not everyone has that entrepreneurial mindset that you really need to succeed in this business."

"She was losing money?" I ask, trying to pin her down on exactly what she knew of Karen's financial situation.

"Robert was upset. They were down four grand including the conference-"

"Thousand? You said that's how much it costs?"

"Well, yeah. It was seven hundred just for the ticket and then the flight and the food. It adds up."

I make a mental note of the fact that Robert said that it was either six or seven hundred and that means that's exactly what he thought it cost or perhaps that's what Karen told him it cost.

"Would you say that this was a major issue in their relationship?"

"I don't know," Elin says. Her demeanor appears rather cagey and I don't believe her. "We were close friends, and I don't want to reveal her secrets."

"You're not gossiping," I encourage her. "I'm trying to find her, and every little bit of information helps me to do that."

"Yeah," she says. She gets up and puts the boxes of candles away. "I'm assuming you don't want to buy one."

"I really can't. I'm working right now," I say and suddenly realize just how awkward this conversation must feel for all of her old friends and relatives who just want to catch up or have a little fun with a friend and end up being marketed candles that they don't really want and that are way overpriced.

Elin walks over to the big window that looks out onto the playground below. Then she opens the door and walks onto the little patio. There's a table made of metal in the corner, along with two chairs and a baby bouncer.

She waves to her husband who walks with his head buried in his phone, pushing the stroller.

"Karen always wanted to have children," she says, pointing to the patio chair.

I take a seat putting the recorder in between us.

"How long have they been married?"

"Five years, I think. Long enough, but he was in graduate school. He was always working. He was always teaching. She said she wanted to do it. She said that she was willing to do it herself, like taking all the baby duties, that kind of thing, but he said he wanted to be around for that. He said he didn't want to miss the first year or two with the baby so they would have to wait, and they did. After he graduated, he still stalled. She's just got this feeling that there is something else going on. A month ago, we spent one Saturday night trailing him."

"Really?"

"Yeah. First, even before she ever told me anything about it, she put a GPS on his car because he would turn off the one on his phone all the time. So, she put one in his car to track him to see where he was going. She just wanted to make sure that he was actually going to work all the times that he's out until, like, midnight. Guess what? He wasn't. He was going to different bars over in Santa Monica and in the Hills. One time, even all the way to Calabasas. It was ridiculous. He acts like this shy engineer guy, but what was he doing going out to all those places? That's what she wanted to find out."

"So, what happened?" I ask.

"She was really upset when she found out. I thought that it was about her sales and how she couldn't recruit anyone in her downline, the people that are salespeople under her, like she's under me. Anyway, she was upset about that, too. She was more upset about her marriage. She was crying. She was inconsolable. I suggested that we follow him. That Saturday night when he said he was working, I got Pete to babysit and we just went out and did it."

"What do you mean by that?" I ask. "What happened?"

11

——————

It gets a little bit cold on the porch as the sun starts to set and Elin offers me something to drink. I follow her to the kitchen as she puts on the kettle. The walls have recently been painted and a few professionally shot photos of the family of three are hanging on the wall. "Tell me about what happened when you followed him," I say.

She pours hot water into two identical West Elm mugs and drops an English breakfast tea bag into mine. The recorder is still running and I watch as the seconds on the front face tick by.

Forty-five.

Forty-six.

Forty-seven.

She clenches her jaw, moves it from side to side as if to release some tension, and then looks up at me.

"It was horrible," she finally says. Elin takes a sip of her tea, shaking her head again, her eyes full of disappointment. "Frankly, I thought it would actually be fun or exciting maybe. It's not that I wanted her husband to be cheating on her, but I've never been involved with anything like that. I'm not a detective, or a PI, or anyone from your world. I just stay home with my kid, take her on play dates, and try to find ways to make a little bit of extra money for our family."

I nod. I take a long sip of my tea and let the warm liquid rush down, warm me up from the inside out.

With the sun setting over the horizon, it suddenly becomes very dark in her apartment. She flips on the light above our heads and luckily it's not fluorescent, but a pleasant, warm candlelit hue that washes over her and gives her a serene kind of look.

She adjusts her bra strap and fidgets to turn around to the refrigerator and look inside. She offers me something to eat, but I quickly say no, waiting for her to continue. She pulls out a half-eaten cake perfectly sliced from the middle out.

"Baking is a passion of mine," she says when I comment on how nice it looks.

There's a thick layer of frosting wrapped perfectly around the circular cake like someone had put a lot of effort into making it. The frosting glistens and shines with colors of turquoise and gold. I lean over and notice a few speckles of gold flakes sprinkled all around.

"You have a real talent."

"Wait until you try it," she says.

I'm about to say no again, but my mouth starts to water and I decide, why not? If she's willing to talk to me and open up, I might as well try a little bit of her cake. She cuts me a piece that is way too generous and grabs one about half that size for herself.

"I really won't be able to eat this much."

"Oh, please, wait until you taste it. I'm sure you will," she says.

"What about you?" I ask.

She shrugs and answers, "Look at me. This baby weight is not going anywhere unless I stop baking and that's probably not going to happen."

"Exactly my point," I joke.

"No, I need to at least try, right? Put in some effort. I'm not even thirty."

I smile. That kind of attitude is not particularly common in Los Angeles, especially since people tend to worship their Pilates classes and their gyms. I appreciate her bluntness and her honesty.

I sit down in her dining table nook and I ask her again about what happened the night they followed Robert.

This time, she opens up.

"She tagged his car, so she knew exactly where he was going. We met up around seven that Saturday night."

"When was this exactly?" I ask.

"I don't remember. Probably about a month ago. Maybe three weeks. Not too long."

"Okay, keep going."

"Well, she could track where the car was going on her phone on this website using his GPS coordinates. She picked me up and we went there together."

"Where did it take you?"

"Up Laurel Canyon all the way to Mulholland Drive and then to Reseda."

"Reseda? Up in the Valley?" I ask.

"Yeah."

"What happened there?"

"He was going to this house. At first, she thought that maybe he was having an affair with some rich girl or something, but it was just this average middle-class kind of house, two bedrooms, one bath. A small pool in the backyard, but nothing extravagant."

"How do you know how big the house is?"

"We drove up there," she says, "and then when we parked outside, I looked it up on Zillow. This woman, she just recently bought it. I can give you the address."

"Did Karen go in?"

"Yes."

"She did?" I ask, surprised.

"Yeah, we waited in the car for a while for him to come out, like an hour. There was an In-N-Out Burger right across the street and I got hungry, so we went there, ate it in the car, fries, Coke, the whole works and then she said, 'That's it.' She was going in."

"What about you?"

"I was going to stay in the car at first, but then I wasn't sure what was going to happen and I didn't want her to get hurt. It was dark. The neighbors started walking their dogs. It wasn't a scary kind of neighborhood at all, kind of pedestrian, actually. I've actually never thought about Reseda before but when I looked up the houses there, it's probably one of the only places where Pete and I can afford to get a house. Of course, it'll be quite a commute for him to get to West LA, but it'll be a nice place for Logan to grow up, right?"

She's getting off track. I can't tell if she's just trying to avoid talking about it or she actually doesn't want me to know. I glance down at my phone. I realize that I've been here way longer than I had planned on and I have to rush this along if I still want to make it to all of the other places I have to go.

At the same time, I know how these types of interrogations go. It's better not to rush things. Sometimes the most mundane details are the ones that become important.

"What happened there? What happened at the house?" I ask.

"She walked up, she knocked, no one answered. She waved me over, I approached as well. She tried the doorknob. They were in the backyard in the pool naked, him and his girlfriend."

"Oh my God, really?"

"Yeah. There's something else," she says quietly.

"What?"

"There was baby stuff all around the house. That woman, Margaret Layne, she had a child, *his* child."

"Really?"

"Yeah. We looked it up later. He told her what her name was and we looked her up on social media and the baby looks just like him. She confronted him about it and he finally admitted it."

"So, what happened? What does this mean then? Were they breaking up?"

"They had all these fights. Their relationship was very complicated. At one point, we stopped talking for a good week or ten days. I think it was because she called and was talking to him again. They were going to be working on their marriage and she didn't want to tell me what was going on."

"Really?" I ask.

She nods and admits, "It's all very toxic, but we had this plan, this business trip, planned a while ago for months. We were going to stay in the same hotel room and all."

"How was the trip?"

"It was good, inspiring. She got really interested in trying to sell the candles again and she made this whole list of all these people she was going to reach out to, like all of her old contacts, old friends, and that kind of thing. The last time I heard from her was when I dropped her off at home. That's it."

"Okay. What happened then? What happened that day?"

"What do you mean?"

"The doctor's appointment?"

"Oh, yeah." Her face falls and she takes another big bite of her cake.

I wait for her to swallow. She plays with her fork for a while, smashing the little bits, the little crumbs into the frosting over and over again.

"I had this terrible feeling when I dropped her off. Maybe it was an ominous kind of thing or whatever, but I just really didn't want to let her go. I remember hugging her so tightly and I even asked her if she wanted to come and stay at our house, but she didn't. She said that she had the doctor's appointment in the morning and she was going to confirm whether or not she was actually pregnant before telling Robert."

"Confirm?" I ask. "She already took a pregnancy test?"

"Yeah, she took about seven. I think she bought one of each at the pharmacy just to make sure and they all came back pregnant, but she wanted to get a blood test from her doctor, and she wanted to do it before telling Robert about it."

"What was she thinking? Was she going to keep it? Was she going to try to make it work with him?"

"I don't know what she was thinking. I think she was just hurt and confused about everything." She chews slowly and then takes the spoon in her tea and stirs, making a loud dinging sound on the sides of the cup.

I don't stay much longer after that. I give her my card and I ask her to call me if she remembers or hears anything else. She promises that she will and she asks me to give her a call as well when I find out anything, anything at all.

I walk back to my car lost in thought. Elin was the one who encouraged Robert to call the police. She was practically the one that made the initial call and he was reluctant to do so.

Does that mean that he was involved? It wouldn't be the first time that a husband killed his wife, especially if she were pregnant with his child and he had already moved on with someone else.

Wait, I'm getting ahead of myself. For now, Karen is just missing. Maybe she just left him. Took off. Took a break.

But if she is dead, it was probably the husband who did it.

Why kill her though? Why kill your wife? Why not just get divorced and move on? Why ruin so many lives in the process?

After all of these years on this job, I feel like people have become even more of an enigma to me than they were when I got started. I thought that I would try to right all the wrongs that came my way and that's what would make this job worth doing, but in reality, there're so many unknowns.

There are so many reasons why people do certain things that make no sense at all and never will. Psychologists try to explain. They try to frame it in the context of who this person is by what they went through and that's why they did this. Most of the time, that hardly makes sense because there are people who live similar lives but don't do half the evil things that others do.

Is Robert one of these people? Elin has her suspicions. As far as motive goes, I guess there's that, too. He had a new girlfriend, new baby, and he wanted to move on, but is that enough for a man like him to kill his wife?

12

I call the doctor's office as I'm running late and ask if she'll still be there fifteen minutes from now. They reschedule me for an hour and a half later, so I decide to swing by the Kaslar apartment building again and see what I can find out from the neighbors, perhaps even their cameras.

I'm lucky with parking and I find a spot directly across from their house. I head to the downstairs neighbor's place first and knock on the door. A young woman who looks to be about nineteen opens, wearing nothing but a bathrobe.

I show her my badge and ask her if she has a few minutes to talk. She says that she's running late to an audition, but I can come in and wait inside. Her apartment is almost identical in layout to the

Kaslars' and I sit down on her frumpy couch
while she changes in her bedroom and comes out
a few minutes later.

She asks me for my name again and sits down
across from me, crossing her legs. I jump right in
and ask her what she knows about her neighbors.

"Yeah, I see Robert around," she says casually
with a little shrug of her shoulders.

"What about Karen?"

"Kind of, just a brief hello here and there."

"So how long have you been living here?"

"About a year. When I moved in, they were very
nice. I think she might've even stopped by with a
pie or something like that, but our schedules are
really different, and I don't see her much."

"She's mainly home, right?"

"I guess so. I'm very busy."

I nod. I can't tell if she's lying or she's trying to
keep something to herself.

"Is there anything else that you can tell me about
them? Did you hear anything suspicious or seen
anything suspicious on Monday, day or night?" I
look at my notepad and give her the precise date.

"No, I wouldn't say that. I was actually not home that day. I had an audition, but it wasn't in LA. It was in Phoenix."

"Would you have any cameras set up anywhere?" I ask.

She shakes her head. I thank her for her time and get up to leave, but she stops me when I get to the door.

"You know that she thought that Robert was cheating on her, right?" she says.

This statement stops me dead in my tracks.

"How do you know that?"

"Well, I kind of overheard her and her friend talking when they were out on the landing. Her friend was kind of this big chubby girl, long hair, and pasty skin."

Elin.

I nod.

"I don't know her name," she says with a shrug, "but I heard them talking about it. They were pretty loud. She was upset."

"When was this?"

"I don't know, like a week ago or something. I was just coming in, bringing some groceries from Trader Joe's and I think the friend was smoking and that's why they were outside, but they were pretty loud. She was really upset."

"What did they say exactly?"

"Just that she suspected something and put something on his car. She wanted her friend to follow him with her."

"To follow Robert?" I ask.

"Yeah."

Okay, so there's some corroboration, I say to myself.

"Was she going to confront him about this?"

"It didn't sound like it. I mean maybe, if she caught him, but it didn't really sound like she would and I saw them afterward, like getting in the car together, going somewhere and everything was very cordial."

"Cordial?" I ask.

"Yeah, you know, friendly but not like perfect though. People get into cars all sorts of ways."

I nod my head and thank her for her time. After giving her my card, I walk out 100% certain that

Elin was telling me the truth. Now the question is when I'm going to confront Robert with it.

I look at the time and realize that I'm running late for my postponed appointment with her OBGYN. I'll interview the rest of the neighbors later. I arrive at the office right on time and the woman at the front desk ushers me to some back room where a woman with a small stature and chopsticks in her hair the way that I used to wear mine back in the nineties gives me a nod. She has perfect skin, a perfect figure, and her white coat is tailored to her body just so.

She introduces herself as Dr. Rothfluss and I catch her up on what I know so far.

"Oh, wow. I can't believe that she's missing. Two days?"

"Yes," I say. "She had an appointment to see you the day of her disappearance. I just wanted to confirm that and whether or not she ever showed up."

"As you know, I can't share her medical records without her consent."

"Yes, of course," I say, "but can you at least confirm whether she had the appointment to see you? Her friend insists that she did and she's not sure if she ever went."

Dr. Rothfluss hesitates. She's not an attorney and it's a big thing to share medical records without the consent of the patient. I can see her wondering whether this is indeed the case in what I'm asking her to do.

"Please," I say, leaning closer to her. "She took about seven or so pregnancy tests and she found out that she was pregnant. Each one confirmed it. She had the appointment to get a blood test at your office and I guess to see you. I just need to know whether this happened or not, not the results of anything."

Dr. Rothfluss nods her head, pulls out her iPad, and scrolls through her records. She licks her lips as she goes through and searches for Karen's name and holds her chin up slightly in the air as she searches.

"Yes, it looks like she did make an appointment at eleven o'clock but she did not show up," she says. "I can't tell you anything else without a court order."

"I understand," I say. "Thank you so much."

"What do you think happened?" Dr. Rothfluss asks. "Do you think she just left?"

"It's hard to tell," I say. "Did you know her personally?"

"She came in here to..." Dr. Rothfluss hesitates.

I know that this is a delicate issue and that it's difficult for her to skirt that line, but I also get the sense that she wants to tell me something.

"Well, we met in a yoga class," she says. "It was that same one that Elin attended. I was Elin's doctor with her baby and she introduced us, so we were sort of on friendly terms."

"Okay, okay, that's good." I nod. "What else?"

"Well, she talked to me personally, not as a doctor but about how much she wanted to have children and her husband didn't, but they were trying, reluctantly."

"What do you mean?"

"Well, I guess they weren't using protection, but he wasn't fully on board with it."

"Oh, okay. Got it. How long had they been trying for?"

"About a year and a half, but from what she told me, as a friend, they were only having sex once every two months, three months, or so. I'm not sure that they were exactly trying."

I give her a nod and agree, "Yeah, that doesn't sound like actually trying. Anyway, when was the last time that you saw her?"

"Probably a week ago. She didn't mention anything about scheduling an appointment and she must've called on her own to my office, but she did mention about wanting to possibly consider IVF."

"She did?" I ask.

"Yeah. This was just when we were in yoga and I tried to tell her that it's unclear whether she would need that kind of intervention because, well, she and her husband were just not being sexually active enough, but she said that she wanted to talk about it."

"Okay. Do you remember precisely what day this was?"

"I don't know, like the fourteenth, maybe? Let me see." She looks at her schedule. "It was the Monday before last."

I nod. I look at my own calendar on my phone and realize that this was right before she caught her husband cheating with Elin.

So, perhaps things have changed since then.

I thank her for her time and leave her office with a lot of thoughts on my mind. The timeline must be that she was trying to get pregnant. She was considering IVF, but she was still suspecting her husband of infidelity.

Then that Saturday, she found out the truth.

The question is what happened between that Saturday and the day that she disappeared?

Did she confront Robert? No, because she was at her conference, but what happened at her conference?

What happened when she appeared? What happened when she came back? She came back that evening and I have to find out whether there are any cameras from any of the neighbors showing her coming and going.

13

I return to their apartment building and knock on a few more doors. Two of the neighbors don't answer, but an older woman who lives downstairs does.

She doesn't welcome me inside but agrees to talk through the half-opened door. I get the sense that she's a bit of a hoarder from what I can see peeking inside and she doesn't want me to see it.

I ask her the same questions I asked Delia, the actress, and she also says that she rarely sees the Kaslars.

The older woman is dressed in sweats, but her face is nicely made up and pulled back, filled up with fillers. She makes a few references to the older model Mercedes parked in front of her apartment and when I finally comment on it, her face beams and she smiles from ear to ear.

"I just bought it," she says. "It's a 2005, but it is a Mercedes."

"Congratulations," I say, knowing that the car couldn't have cost more than three thousand dollars. "Does it run well?"

"Of course it runs well. What kind of question is that?" She gasps.

I realize that was a mistake. I apologize quickly, but it doesn't seem to reverse her scorn toward me.

"Mrs. Ossap, I'm really just trying to get to the bottom of what happened to Karen. The last that we know is that she came back from a business trip, but now she's missing and no one has seen her for two days. I was just wondering if you remember anything," I plead and appeal to her because I need her help.

She hesitates for a moment and it looks like she's about to slam the door in my face.

"Listen, I told you about my car."

"Yes, I understand," I say.

"No, you don't." She shakes her head. "I know that a lot of people are interested in it, even though you may not be."

I nod, not entirely sure about where this is going.

"You know, it still means something to drive a Mercedes," Mrs. Ossap says. "To make sure that no one damages it, or accidentally bumps into it, I set up some surveillance equipment."

"You did?" I gasp.

She looks like she is in her eighties and I had no idea that people of that age knew how to set this kind of stuff up.

"Yes, my grandson was going to do it, but he was asking me about my will and he was really just generally getting on my nerves, expecting me to give him money that he doesn't deserve. So, I did it myself."

"Would you mind showing me what you have?" I ask.

She crosses her arms and shakes her head.

"Please, Mrs. Ossap, you may have the key to her disappearance."

"Okay, fine, but only because you apologized." She points her manicured finger in my face, the tips are pointy, long, and kind of remind me of Cardi B's, which is another incongruous thing for a woman of her age to have.

People are strange.

She waves me inside and finally lets me into her space. There are boxes of things from floor to ceiling, but only in the front. When I walk past the narrow hallway in between the boxes, it opens up to a rather spacious, minimalist style living room. It's like she wants other people to think that she's this crazy old cat lady hoarder but in reality, she's got this sleek, perfect little space that looks like it belongs in the pages of a Pottery Barn catalog.

She walks me over to a big computer table made of glass with a Mac desktop positioned in the center. She clicks around and opens the files with the recordings.

"Wow, you have quite a setup here," I say.

"I work online."

"You do?"

"Yeah."

"What is it that you do?"

"I'm a photographer. For many years back in the sixties I did black and white fashion photography, but then men dominated that business and it was hard to get through. Now, finally, I'm getting the recognition I deserve. I have social media and I have a website. I have a lot of clients and my photographs have appeared in *Vogue, National Geographic*, and lots of online magazines. Recently, I've been doing a lot of real people portraits. I'd like to do one of you."

I hesitate.

"I've never done one of a cop before."

"It would be unprofessional for me to do that given that I'm on this case and I'm interviewing you for work."

"Yeah, I get it," she says. "Well, how about after the case? Would you consider it?"

"Yes. I've never actually had a professional picture taken before," I say.

"You're missing out. I'd love to show you the ropes," she says.

I steer her attention back to Karen and she shows me the surveillance videos. Thankfully, she keeps them all for a month, just in case. She scrolls over to the date and time that I tell her. We try in the evening and I see Karen coming back home, looking tired while pulling a suitcase behind her.

She scrolls through her phone as she walks and then disappears upstairs.

I ask Mrs. Ossap to see if she has any surveillance of later that day. We scroll through. Neighbors come and go but none of them are Karen or Robert.

"Is this the only exit out of the building?"

I scroll through again just to make sure that I didn't miss anything, but neither Robert nor Karen seem to enter or leave the building.

"Yes, but I don't have any cameras out there."

I bite my lower lip. That could be a problem.

I keep scrolling and then suddenly, in the corner, I see a figure. I pause and then slow it down. It's shadowy, but it resembles Robert. I look at the time. Four p.m., right around the time that he was supposed to come back home, but when I look closer, I realize that it's not him at all. This guy has long hair and for a moment, he comes into full visibility. He doesn't look anything like him.

"What are you looking for exactly?" she asks, sitting back in the executive chair. "You think that he killed his wife and dragged her body out the front in daylight?"

"I don't know. Maybe. What do you think could have happened?"

"I didn't hear any sounds, so if he did kill her, he must have done something quiet. Did you check his apartment?"

"No. Not yet."

"Why?"

"Probable cause. I don't have any."

"What do you mean?" she asks.

"I need to get a warrant, or he needs to let me do it, but so far, at least when I was there, I didn't see anything too glaring that would draw my attention that would allow a judge to give me a warrant."

"Well, sorry that I couldn't be more helpful," she says.

Before leaving, I ask her to send me these recordings to my email address just so they don't get erased. I want to go through them again and see if maybe there was anything that I could have missed. Maybe the forensics team would spot a detail that I overlooked.

She agrees and then makes me promise that she can take my picture for her portrait gallery. She starts to show me some of her work, but I glance at the time and say that I can't stay.

"Okay. Well, I'll be in touch," she says, holding up my card in between her fingers. "Don't think that you'll get away so quickly."

"I don't even know why you want to take my picture," I say. "I'm not exactly model material."

"Oh, that's what you think, huh? That's not what photographers want. Photographers want a face with character, someone who expresses their discontent with life, and you can clearly see it."

"Is that what I express?" I ask, furrowing my brow, not sure if I should take it as a compliment or an insult.

"You got something to say. Let's put it that way," she says.

"What?"

"I don't know yet. I haven't taken your picture."

I walk back out to the parking lot with the weight of the world on my shoulders and then, just as I'm considering whether or not to call Robert in for somewhat of an informal conversation at the precinct, I see him.

He parks the car in the back lot and walks up the stairs, carrying about ten bags of groceries, five in each hand. He's not making another trip if it breaks his back.

I walk up to him and offer to help, but everything is balanced in his hands and if he lets go of one thing, everything else might fall as well. So, instead, he just asks me to grab the keys out of his jacket pocket and open the door.

"So, I guess you didn't find her yet," Robert says, putting all of the grocery bags onto the linoleum floor, checkered in alternating black and white.

"No, we didn't, but I've been making the rounds, asking a lot of questions, and I actually have some things to follow up with you."

He opens the refrigerator and starts to unpack his groceries. He seems completely unbothered by the fact that his wife is gone. As a detective, you sometimes fall into the trap of trying to read body language for clues as to what might have or might not have happened, but time and time again, various professionals and psychologists have concluded that body language experts and body language science in general is nothing but fake science.

The thing is that there is no one way that people react to situations. We all know this, but we still expect people to have certain reactions to certain news. The people who study this sort of thing conclude that body language is impossible to read mainly because it is so culturally specific.

Certain cultures encourage expression of emotions. Others don't. Furthermore, people grow up in different families. In some families, emotions are freely talked about and in others they are repressed and tucked away, never to be spoken about. That's what makes it such a difficult thing to do and therefore, it is not a scientific body of influence at all but rather filled with people just making statements for the sake of making statements.

I stand in Robert's kitchen and he continues to ignore me. After a few minutes, I start to feel physically uncomfortable. I'm waiting for him to say something in response to my presence, but he doesn't. He just focuses himself on this mindless task of putting away groceries and that's it.

"Tell me about your girlfriend," I say to snap him to attention and his spine immediately becomes rigid. I watch the back of his neck and see little hairs stand up on end.

"There, I got his attention," I say silently to myself.

"What girlfriend?" he asks, after relaxing his face. He doesn't look perplexed or upset but rather indignant.

"You know, the one who Karen caught you with in her house in Reseda."

His face turns white. He swallows hard, then clears his throat, avoiding eye contact with me the whole time.

"Why are you here?"

"I'm looking for your wife."

"Yeah. Well, she's not in this apartment, is she?"

"I need answers to these questions, Mr. Kaslar."

"I told you to call me Robert," he snaps.

"Okay, Robert. I need answers."

"I didn't do anything," he mumbles.

"What happened in Reseda?"

"Nothing. That was just nothing. That was just a friend."

"You were swimming naked with her in her pool when your wife came in."

"That was a setup."

"How was that exactly?" I ask.

"She wasn't supposed to be there. It was a one-time thing."

I realize that he's going in circles and now I suddenly wish that he were at the precinct, being recorded saying all of these things. The problem is that I'm not sure if I could get him to admit any of this in that formal environment. The whole thing is that I have the element of surprise.

He hesitates, shifts his weight from one foot to another, but I wait. I can feel that the silence is now uncomfortable for him and that's good. That's exactly what I want.

"Listen. I have no idea what this has to do with anything."

"Did you have an affair or not?"

"Yes, so what? It was a one-time thing. She caught me doing it. Whatever. Do you know how many guys in my department have slept with their teaching assistants? You don't even know what it's like to be married to Karen. She's anal about everything. She is completely obsessive."

"What about the baby?"

"What about the baby? What baby?" he slips.

He first asked what about the baby and then followed up with what baby. That pregnancy was supposed to be a surprise, but clearly, it's not.

"You knew about the pregnancy?"

"No, of course not."

"She took seven pregnancy tests, and she didn't tell you once? You guys were trying to have a baby."

"We were not."

"Were you using protection?"

"She told me she was on the pill."

I walk over to the bathroom.

"Where are you going?" he asks while following behind me.

I open the medicine cabinet and he looks inside.

"What?"

"Most women either carry their pill boxes with them or leave them here in the medicine cabinet. What does she do?" I ask him.

"I don't know. I'm never here. I work all the time."

"Well, according to her friend, you two were

trying to have a baby. In fact, she'd even discussed IVF, in vitro fertilization."

"What? No. No. There's no way. That causes you to have like twins and triplets. We can't afford that."

"So, that was the problem in your marriage? Finances?"

"No, of course not. Stop putting words in my mouth," he says, throwing his hands up. "Why don't you go find my wife, okay? What about her phone? Were you able to trace anything?"

"No. Her phone doesn't ping anywhere," I say, remembering what the crime scene tech team told me a few hours ago. "No evidence. They traced the number and they couldn't find it anywhere."

"What does that mean?" he asks.

"It must be off, but you probably know that already."

"What are you even talking about?"

"What happened to Karen?" I ask, pushing forward.

I stand close to him. I realize that I'm not the most intimidating figure, but I hope that my job title is enough.

He doesn't take the bait though. Sometimes people don't, but you have to try.

"I had nothing to do with Karen's disappearance. I already told you that. I came home. She wasn't here. What more do you want me to say?"

"Okay, Mr. Kaslar. I'll be interviewing some more people and I'll be in touch. Meanwhile, I got some video footage from your neighbors, so I'll be going over that as well."

His face drops. It's like all the blood in his face rushes away from him and he turns an unusual color of blue-green. I wait for a moment for him to say something, but he just clears his throat and looks away.

I walk out, knowing that he's worried about possibly being on that camera footage.

There're a few more people that I have to interview who weren't home earlier, but I have to get back to the precinct and file a report about everything that I've found so far.

I look at the time. It's running out.

14

I get back to the precinct late that night. Most people have already left, but I stay at my desk for a while, trying to get everything done that normally would take two days. I need to be in Captain Medvil's good graces before I ask him for more time off to go back home and search for my sister.

Every day feels a little bit like a twilight zone. I split my time between LA and the small mountain town where I grew up, only there's nothing bucolic or wonderful about it this time. I'm not a visitor. I'm not trying to get away from the traffic or the hustle and bustle of the Southern California valley below. This time I go there to search for ghosts. When I get home, I decide to take a bath. I haven't taken one in years, but something about it calls to me. I light some candles, a birthday present from Sydney from only a month ago, but it feels like it was years.

In addition to the candles, Sydney had presented me with a bamboo table big enough to fit a phone and an iPad to go over the bathtub, one of those things people always have in movies at fancy hotels where you get into a large soaking tub and forget all of your problems.

My apartment is a lightyear away from that life, but when I put the shelf over the tub, throw in some bath bombs, lower the lights, grab my iPad, and open a book I have been reading for close to two weeks, the world falls away. For a good half an hour, I find myself somewhere in another world, worried about a duke and his bride with a disapproving father who refuses to let them marry. I like stories like these, set in lands far away in other worlds where murders don't happen, where DNA doesn't exist, and where people have problems that are very dissimilar from my own.

I let my body relax and I lay my head against a towel folded up into a makeshift pillow. I let my eyes slowly close and my mind drift away. I don't know how much time has passed when I wake up, but I get somewhat of a rude awakening when my nose drops below the level of the water and I breathe in and choke. I splash some water on my face and then lather up some shampoo and wash my hair. Bubbles fill up the tub, mixing with the old ones from the bath bomb. I rinse it out, trying to get the last bit of the shampoo without much success when my phone rings.

It's Captain Talarico from Big Bear Sheriff's Station.

"Any news?" I ask, knowing fully well that he wouldn't be calling me otherwise. It's after midnight and I wonder if he's on his way home, tucked into bed, or still at the office.

"The search found nothing out of the ordinary," he says.

My mom had already messaged that to me, but I wasn't fully convinced until I heard it from him.

"Nothing at all? Not even like a shirt or-"

"Nothing," he says. "Volunteers have turned in a few things, but none of them belonged to her according to your mother and nothing out of the ordinary was found."

"This could be good news or bad news," I say.

"Yes."

"What about Natalie?"

"Bad news. No one has seen her in twenty-four hours. Due to the circumstances under which she has gone missing and the fact that they match your sister's, we are getting the FBI involved. Tomorrow morning, they'll be here."

"So, she's gone, too?"

"Yeah, conducting a search tomorrow around her house as well, same time as your sister's. You'll be here, right? Noon?"

"Yeah. I'll be there."

"Okay. See you then." He hangs up before I can say goodbye.

I stare at my phone. I tuck my legs up to my chest and wrap my arms around them, trying to make the tepid water last a little longer.

Natalie's missing and so is Violet. Now that the FBI's involved, I can't help but wonder which one of the girls is going to get more attention.

Natalie is from a prominent family, lives in a big house with married parents and two brothers who are probably all stricken with grief; and then there's my mom, in her little seventies bungalow, in her old car, and her inability to even appear on camera to showcase her grief publicly in order to get people to care about her daughter.

Sometimes, I hate the way the world works. Sometimes, I hate that certain people, just by the virtue of who they are, get more attention, but the problem is that there's a competition for resources on achieving attention.

I'm going to focus on the positive. Since Natalie is missing now, there's more of a reason to search for both of them. There'll be more media attention and perhaps more answers.

I climb out of the bath and pull out the plug, wrapping myself in a towel and feeling colder than I ever did before I got in. I see that I have a missed call from Luke and I'm tempted to call him back, but I don't know him well and the person that I'm going to be on the phone with him right now is not going to be pleasant, sweet, or someone he'd want to take on a second date.

I climb into bed and try to get a few hours of shuteye before embarking on another long day and seeking answers to questions that may not have any.

I get to the office a little bit after six a.m. and fuel myself with a donut and coffee. The sugar speeds up my heartbeat and gives me a fake jolt of energy that I know is going to wear off in a few hours and make my stomach growl, but when I see it, I can't resist.

When I get to my desk, I see that the lights in Captain Medvil's office are already on. He likes to get here early and usually leaves a little bit early to get home and spend some time with his wife.

I walk by and say hello. He immediately asks me for details on the Kaslar case. I have submitted a report, but I go over the details verbally. It's faster this way.

He nods while listening and asks what the plan of action will be.

"I want to invite him in. I want to do a proper interview. He admitted to the affair. He somewhat admitted to the pregnancy, but if we can get him on tape and maybe get him to admit a few more things, that will be ideal."

"You still have no body."

"I have no idea where she is."

"What about the videotapes?" He still calls them that, even though they have long been digital recordings.

"The ones I got from Mrs. Ossap downstairs, they were useless. I led him on to think that maybe we had something and I'd like to keep that to myself or between us, but there was nothing on them. There was a guy that looked like him, but then there was a close-up. It turned out to not be him at all."

"Are you sure it's not just him in disguise?"

"Yeah. I have it in my email. I'll forward them to you and to the tech team, but I'm pretty sure it's not him."

"So, no body, still missing, two days now, friend worried, concerned that he might have done something, but when and how? We wouldn't be able to get a warrant with what we have so far," he says, thinking out loud. "So, unless he admits something in the interview, we don't have much to go on, but you seriously think that this guy could have done something to her?"

"No, I didn't say that. I mean, he's very shady, cruel, and crude, but it was daytime, and they live in an apartment building. There were no gun shots fired, and there's still no body."

"He could have strangled her."

"Yeah, but then what? What did he do with the body?"

"We have to check those cameras."

"There's another exit," I say with a heavy heart.

"What do you mean?"

"There's another exit to the apartment building, one that goes out back. There are no cameras there."

"Ugh," he growls.

WHEN I GET to Big Bear the following morning, I get there just in time to go to the search. Much to my surprise, Luke is there, along with Captain Talarico running the show. Captain Talarico introduces us, but I tell him that we have already met without going over any of the details.

When he told me last night that they were going to get the FBI involved, I had no idea that meant that it would be Luke Gavinson.

When a deputy comes up to the captain to ask him a few things, his attention is diverted and I pull Luke aside.

We're standing under a makeshift tent. There are picnic tables, laptops, and a generator set up even though these are the outside headquarters of the search.

The local veterans' hall was kind enough to give us the space to set up a makeshift headquarters for the search. There are tables all along the wall with volunteers. Luckily, my mom was involved enough to organize some aspect of this, even though she had trouble with going on the actual search. She had big posters made of the missing sign, along with blown-up photos of Violet smiling, laughing, and having fun.

I stare at one of the pictures in which her hair is braided and I'm surprised at how different she looks. Perhaps photographers are onto something when they say they want to capture the essence of that person. Most of the time it seems to be something serious, different, unpleasant, maybe even unattractive, unless of course it's a glossy fashion magazine, but as I look around at these pictures of my sister, I realize that none of them really represent her. They express the best versions of her, the fun, outgoing side, but that part of her has always been small in comparison to the moody darkness that often enveloped her. She was serious, bookish, and not really outgoing at all.

When I glance at the poster of the other missing girl, her friend Natalie D'Achille, I realize that the story has to be about their similarities. Nobody wants to look for an introvert. Nobody wants to look for somebody who even has a hint of darkness to them. They become a villain, especially in the superficial, surface only society, media saturated culture in which we live.

"What are you doing here?" I ask Luke after a deputy walks past us talking frantically on the phone to one of his children.

"I was assigned here, but it's good to see that you're so glad to see me," he jokes, but only partly.

His dark hair falls slightly onto his face, on his high cheekbones, and on his strong jaw. It makes me want to kiss him right here, right now, even though it would be the most unprofessional thing that I could do.

"You look nice in that suit," he says, pointing to my pencil skirt and blouse. I smile while my new bra digs deep into my back, making me extremely uncomfortable.

"I thought you'd be a little bit less dressed up," he adds, pausing for a moment.

"Well, I'm trying to look professional, even though this is in your jurisdiction. Maybe I'll get another reporter to do a story. Who knows?"

"Well, you look nice, even though I know you hate it."

"Thank you," I say and wait for him to answer my question.

"I just got a call this morning to come down here, had to take an early flight. Thought I'd surprise you."

I nod, moving my jaw from one side to another.

"Listen, I didn't ask to be assigned to this case, if that's what you're asking."

"No, I'm not."

"It's just a coincidence. Things weren't going that great up north anyway."

I'm tempted to ask what happened, but I have too many cases and too many other people's problems going through me right now.

Captain Talarico waves us over from across the hall and I quickly glance over at Luke to make sure that we are maintaining the proper distance from one another. No one here can know that we're together. It's completely unprofessional, even though I'm not officially assigned to the case. It would be a problem since I am one of the victim's sister, but I'm glad he's here and I'm glad I have a friend to talk to.

The search is starting and I meet my mom out in front of the search headquarters. She's dressed in jeans and a hoodie and looks tired, but a little less bewildered than before.

"How was everything yesterday?" I ask, introducing Luke as Agent Gavinson.

"We're here to help you, Mrs. Carr," Luke says.

My mom looks up and down at his suit, his silk tie, and the pressed white collar. She looks completely unimpressed.

"You all act like you want to help us and we should trust you," Mom says, "but the FBI isn't anything."

"Mom," I gasp, "what are you doing? He's here to help us. We're lucky to have them involved."

"Lucky?" Mom narrows her eyes. "No, I'm not lucky, Kaitlyn. I'm anything but that. My daughter is missing and you're here acting like it's supposed to be some big deal that the FBI is involved."

I clench my jaw and pull her aside, apologizing silently to Luke who just waves his hands like it's nothing and walks away to give us space.

"I want them to find my daughter," Mom snaps.

She pulls out a cigarette and takes a drag. The crisp cold air makes the smoke dance in front of her, but the bright sunshine also sheds light onto the thin spindly wrinkles around her mouth that years of sucking on cigarettes have formed. Her skin is almost yellow and devoid of any rouge or color. She has had better days and I know it as much as she does.

"Listen, whatever your thoughts are about the FBI, keep them to yourself. They're here to help, okay? There's another girl missing and the two cases might be connected."

"What do I care about that?" she asks, taking another puff and blowing the smoke in my face.

"What do you mean?"

"Her friend, Natalie, who lied about where she was that night or at least covered up for her boyfriend? What do I care where she is, Kaitlyn? Why do you? All that matters is Violet and now that that other skank is involved, that girl who comes from that nice family, with that big house across the way, no one's going to look for Violet as much as they'll look for her."

"They will if you don't alienate them," I say, gritting through my teeth. "They will if you clean up, you look nice, you plead for people's help, and you're grateful for people who come to help you, who really don't have to be here."

"Oh, please."

"Mom, she's a missing person. She's thirteen and there's some evidence that she might have just run away. Okay? Police, they like to believe those stories about teenage girls because that clears cases off their desks. That's better than looking for

some phantom, a ghost, which is what she is now.
So please, don't make this more difficult than it
has to be. Okay? I want Violet found. You want
her found. The police, the FBI, everybody wants
her found. Let's all work together."

Mom turns her face away from me, but I can tell
that I'm getting through. I walk away from her
and suddenly I feel like a teenager again, annoyed
and pissed off, with a desire to hit something really
hard. There's this angst building within me. I hate
everything that she stands for, how she treats me
and Violet, and yet doesn't seem to rise to the
standard of me cutting her off.

The problem is that my mom is just desperate and
sad enough to keep me stringing along every time
I talk to her. It was the same way when I was in
college, when I moved to New York and she would
call me about every little problem and keep me on
the phone without letting me hang up.

Anyone else probably would have or should have,
but I was eighteen years old and I couldn't force
myself to push her away. I still needed her as a
mother. Now? Now I need her again. Violet is still
a kid and as long as she's under eighteen, I have to
keep things cordial with my mom.

15

The search starts and I purposely separate myself from my mom and participate in another small pod of people. There are deputies that make assignments, giving us the usual warnings about not touching anything and taking pictures of anything unusual or suspicious.

Mom goes with a group of three elderly ladies and I join the one with twenty somethings of which I quickly discover are teachers at their school.

"I just can't believe that your sister's missing," Sarah Applegate says, grabbing my hand.

She is a peppy, outgoing woman with thick curls and a generous amount of lip gloss and mascara. She teaches math and though she's never had

Violet, she has seen her around and felt like it was her duty to join the search.

"You're a detective, right?" Eliza Deal asks, getting on the other side of me as we're looking at the quadrants that we have been assigned to.

Nothing has been laid out or mocked up. They're just estimates of space around you where you have to focus your gaze in order to make sure that no one misses a thing.

"Yeah. I'm her older sister," I say, giving both of them my card.

"So, what do they think happened? What do you think happened?"

"I'm not officially on the case since this isn't my jurisdiction, but we have no idea. Have you heard anything? Have you seen anything? Did anyone happen to say anything unusual about her?"

It's not ideal to talk to them under these circumstances because during a search, you have to really focus on the ground in front of you but it's also in these kind of circumstances when people tend to open up and I don't want to shut down any possible information either.

I tell them the last time that she was seen and the circumstances under which she disappeared. They both tilt their heads sympathetically.

Eliza was her homeroom teacher a few times, a rotating position where different teachers come in early morning, take roll, and organize kids and have them sit in the same classroom for about half an hour before classes officially start.

"She always sat somewhere in the middle," Eliza says. "A few times I subbed for her homeroom teacher. She always listened to her AirPods and it seemed like she was trying to catch up on homework that she hadn't gotten to."

"She was a good student, right?" I ask.

"Yes, by all accounts. As and Bs mostly, but recently she'd started to slip up."

"Oh, what do you mean?" I ask, stopping in my tracks. Now I definitely won't be able to pay attention to the search, but I want to know more about this.

"A friend of mine teaches English, Miss Dolores. She was mentioning how the last quarter she'd stopped turning in assignments, was always distracting kids in class, and just not doing what she was supposed to. It was unusual because she'd had her the year before and she wasn't like that at all."

"Oh, wow. Okay. I'll have to talk to her," I say. "Miss Dolores, you said?"

"Yes, Catherine Dolores. English."

I write down her name in my notebook and show them, to check the spelling. I had always assumed that what Violet told me about her classes and what even Mom told me about her schoolwork was true, but suddenly I'm starting to have doubts.

If someone had interviewed my mom when I was in middle school, she would have also told them that I was mostly an A, B student, but in reality, I was forging transcripts and lying about my grades.

We continue with the rest of our search grid-by-grid. I ask them a few more questions, but that seems to be the extent of what they know since they have only peripheral knowledge of her work. Now however, I'm more certain than ever that I have to conduct more thorough interviews with her teachers and guidance counselors along with getting her school records to see what exactly was going on with her.

When I get back to the search headquarters, I find Luke stuffing his face with a donut. He was catching up on the case, reading all the files and the interviews, and didn't actually participate in the search.

"How was it?"

"I didn't find anything. I guess we'll see if anyone else did. Do you want to grab something to eat?" I ask.

"Yes. More than anything." He smiles. "I've already had two of these and I'm afraid the third one is going to put me in hyperglycemia shock."

16

I take Luke to Social 21, which is kind of a hipster restaurant bar on the main town boulevard. There are heat lamps set up outside and a bunch of cool twenty-somethings who know just the right cocktail to order, are parked under heat lamps and around the outside fire pits.

"Wow, this is unusual. I had no idea you had such a cool place here," he says.

"Yeah, this one caters to the LA audience and the food is quite exceptional."

The hostess takes us to a table for two in the back, underneath a flat big heat lamp that isn't really even that necessary since it's almost seventy degrees outside.

"Listen, I want to apologize," he says after we order a round of cocktails. It's not something we're supposed to do while we're on the clock, but I'm not officially working and he decides to go for it anyway.

"What are you talking about?" I ask.

"About showing up here without warning you. I didn't request this job specifically, but I had a choice from a few and this one would bring me to you and would be the best for my career. So that's what I decided to do."

"I just hope that you can find her," I say, suddenly choking back tears.

"Listen, I'm going to do everything I can. I'm meeting with the D'Achille family in a couple of hours."

"Is there anything else that you can tell me that I should know?"

We order our food. I eat tacos and fried avocados, which is a specialty and one of my favorites. My elderberry cocktail infused with lime arrives and we make a tentative toast to finding my sister.

He makes me believe that I'll be able to find her and even though a part of me knows that it may not be true, I go with it anyway. Sometimes hope is all you have, but it's the most important thing. We try to talk about something else, a different case, music, a movie we might have both seen, but none of the conversations stick.

"That's the thing about being workaholics and being obsessed with our jobs. It's the only thing that we think about. It's the only thing that makes everything worth it, but it also makes you a bad date."

"Why would you say that?" Luke asks, leaning back in his chair when I share my epiphany.

"Don't you feel like that? Don't you feel like all you ever talk about is police work? Like, maybe there's something else going on in the world."

"There's something else going on in the world besides solving murder cases and missing persons cases? Wait, like what exactly?" He laughs and I laugh along with him. "No, seriously though. I get it. That's probably why I haven't had a relationship last more than a year."

"What was she like?" I ask.

We haven't talked of exes yet. That conversation is still looming somewhere over our every interaction.

"Isn't that bad etiquette?" he asks. "I think I must have read that somewhere."

"What, to talk about your exes?"

"Yeah."

"No, I don't think so." I shake my head and pop a fried avocado square into my mouth, letting it melt, biting through its crispy shell and then letting the inside practically melt.

"Hey, I want to know what kind of girls you dated before me."

"Is that where we are? Are we dating?"

"No," I say quickly. "We're just friends."

"Friends. Do you see a lot of your friends naked?"

I laugh. He takes a sip. He finishes his drink and orders another round. I shake my head.

"This isn't really the right time and place," he says after a long pause.

"I know, but I want to think about something besides our jobs and clearly neither of us have seen a movie in a really long time. So, exes are all we have."

He smiles, chuckles to himself, and finally explains, "Okay. My ex-girlfriend and I were together for two years. Well, a year officially and then off and on again before that."

"Was she in law enforcement?"

"No, that was kind of the problem. At first the hours were okay. She stayed busy with her work. She worked in PR, but after a while she just couldn't handle it. We'd have a date or plans to meet with her friends to go out and I'd be on call and I'd have to cancel. It gets tiring after a while. Not everyone can put up with that sort of thing."

"Did you ever think about getting married?"

"She wanted to. That was kind of another problem. She said that it wouldn't be a problem if we got married and we had kids, but I have a crazy job and I want to be there for my kids. I'm not going to be one of those dads that's just working all the time, who's only there for pictures and some important holidays. No, I want to be there from the beginning, even change diapers."

"Well, how's that going to work with your job?" I ask.

"Not sure yet. Not sure how long I'm going to be working."

"Really? What do you mean?" I ask, shaking my head. "You have your whole career ahead of you."

"It's probably not good to talk about it."

"It's fine. I'm not going to say anything if that's what you're worried about."

"Just haven't been feeling it for a while. Just a lot of darkness and paperwork. I think life should be about something more than that."

"Darkness and paperwork." I laugh. "I don't think our career choices have ever been summed up more accurately than that."

"Well, I've had a lot of time to think about what it is that I don't like about my job."

"So, what about transferring? Maybe it's the office. Maybe it's your location. Your boss."

He shakes his head and admits, "I've worked in a few places. It's just, I'm not cut out for this. Guys who do this kind of work they're really into playing cops and robbers. They like catching bad guys. They like to be that version of themselves. Me, not so much. I kind of fell into this and have been doing it for a few too many years and now I'm just trying to figure out what else I can do before I make it official."

"So, what about my sister's case?" I ask.

"I'm going to work it as hard as I can. I'm going to find out who did it. Who took her." He corrects himself to not make it sound so much like someone had actually killed her.

I swallow hard.

"I'll work on this case as long as it takes, Kaitlyn, but that's probably going to be it for me."

17

It throws me off a bit when Luke tells me about wanting to quit his job. People tend to change their jobs a lot outside of law enforcement but within the small insular community, it's all about rising within your rank, upping your pay grade, and getting enough years under your belt in order to get a comfortable retirement. The thought of someone retiring early, I've never heard of that.

"What do you think you want to do?" I ask.

"I don't know. I don't really have many skills. Outside of this, I'm not sure what I'd be qualified to do, but I have certain dreams."

"Dreams?" I ask. I raise my eyebrow and suddenly my attention is focused. "What do you mean by that?"

"I don't know." He shrugs. "It's just thoughts. Don't you have dreams?"

I think about that for a moment.

"For many years, being a detective was all I ever wanted to do," I say quietly.

"What about now?"

"I don't know. It's weird when you're living your best life and you deal with death and missing people all day long. You start to wonder, "Is this all there is?""

"Yeah, that's kind of how I felt," Luke says. "Besides, I wasn't lying when I said that we broke up because I didn't want to be an absentee dad. I'm not judging any other men in this profession, or women, but for me, what I want is more, everything. I want to be there for my baby. I want to be there for all the nights and all the days and see them grow into a person. I don't want to miss that stuff. I want to go to the playgrounds and the soccer games."

"Your career is not that important?" I ask.

"It was for many years, but there are other things that I like to do."

"Like what?"

"Woodworking, music, fighting even."

"Wow. So, like hobbies?" I ask, half joking.

"Yeah, hobbies, I guess. It seems sort of inappropriate to call them that if that's actually what you want to spend your time doing. I have interests and I want to have a job that allows for them a lot more than this one does."

"Well, I don't know if you're looking for a sugar mama, but you know what my pay grade is and I can't exactly say you opened a nice lifestyle," I say, taking a bite of my fish taco.

"Who's saying anything about you being my sugar mama?" He laughs and leans over, pressing his lips to mine.

We kiss for the first time in days.

After we finish the meal, I expect us to get back into the car, but instead he just points to the Robin Hood Resort on the corner and we walk down the picturesque main street with lights wrapped around poles and beautifully landscaped bushes in between various little shops. There's my favorite store that sells homemade fudge and ice cream so I invite him inside to show him the goodies.

The whiff of chocolate and sugar overwhelms the senses as soon as you get inside and Luke's mouth immediately starts to water as he leans over the glass enclosure to look at the fudge, the chocolate eclairs, the chocolate covered cherries, and almonds, and other goodies in all different shades of chocolate, in all the different shades of brown.

I order a quarter pound of chocolate covered cranberries and he gets cordial cherries that are perfectly round balls, a four pack. The woman across the counter asks us if we are also interested in their homemade waffle cones and pistachio ice cream, but we force ourselves to decline.

Luke bites into one before we even close the door and step outside.

"This is amazing," he says, chewing with his mouth open. I pop a chocolate covered cranberry into mine and let the explosion and taste of sweetness mixed with bitterness and a bit of tartness overwhelm my senses.

Robin Hood Resort has a carving of two big bears out front, at least five feet tall each and a small parking lot. It hovers somewhere between a hotel and a motel with doors that go straight outside, but with a few amenities like breakfast and whirlpool spas in the rooms to make it a little bit more upscale. There's no tacky sign advertising the prices or whether or not there's a vacancy and everything about the small lobby makes it look quaint but cared for.

The elderly woman at the front waves to us as we walk by and he asks for another key because he has forgotten his.

"Well, that's not a good sign," I whisper to him while we wait.

The woman up front types into the computer and looks up once to ask him to sign the enormous leather-bound book right in front of him and explains, "This is our guest book and we'd love it if you wrote your name, where you're from, and what brought you here."

I make a little face at him knowing full well that he can't exactly write the truth in there.

Two thirteen-year-old girls have recently gone missing in your picturesque little town, and the sheriff's department brought in the FBI to help investigate.

I lean over his shoulder and look at his little chicken scrawl, barely making out the phrase in the reason line.

A few minutes later, he opens the freshly painted green door to his room and he wraps his arms around my waist as soon as the door slams shut. The light see-through curtains are still closed but letting in just enough light to let me see his body, his face, and the way that his eyes twinkle when they look at me.

He presses his lips to mine and pulls me tight against him. We're both dressed in professional clothing, constricted and tight without much pull. I reach over his shoulders and pull his suit jacket off, letting it slip off his arms.

I run my fingers up and down his toned muscular arms and watch his hands make their way around my neck to tilt my chin up and to kiss me again and again.

A few minutes later, he pulls off my skirt and I unbutton his shirt. We fall into bed together and we don't even bother to turn on the light.

Afterward, lying in his arms in a state of contentment and ecstasy, I look at the time and know that we can't stay here long. I have to get back to the search headquarters. I have to talk to the captain.

"You know no one can know about this, right?" I ask, tilting my head up to look at him from the crook of his arm.

"Of course, I'd be in as much trouble as you, actually, probably more."

"This wasn't a great idea. I mean, we shouldn't have done that."

"Are you saying that because of work or are you saying that because of us?" he asks, suddenly looking very vulnerable and surprised.

I'm tempted to ask what we're doing. I'm tempted to try to define this relationship, if we can even call it that.

My mind is cloudy with so many different tasks and uncertainties. I don't want to add an argument with Luke to that.

"I like you," I say. "A lot."

I lean over and give him a kiss.

When I pull away, he grabs my arm and pulls me closer and kisses me again, harder and more passionately. "I guess you like me, too?" I ask with a smile.

"You could say that." He winks and we both know that it's time to get back.

I use his comb to brush my hair and tie it up in a neat ponytail. We look at one another and check each other's clothes for any irregularities, smoothing the few wrinkles.

I turn to him and ask, "So was forgetting something in your hotel room just a ploy to get me into bed?"

He narrows his eyes, tilts his head to one side, and asks, "What do you think?"

"I think it was, I think it worked."

"I'm not that smooth. I'm not very good at being a player."

"Is that not what all players say?" I joke.

"I actually forgot my laptop here. I thought it was in my briefcase, but it wasn't. That's what I wanted to get." He points to the laptop sitting neatly on the desk next to the television.

I glance at the wire to make sure that it's plugged in and it is, making it difficult to stage.

"Well, either way it kind of worked out," I say, giving him a peck on the cheek and telling him to wait a few minutes before following me out.

When we get back to the VFW, I check the time again and see that we've only been gone two hours. Now, that's what I call a quickie.

As soon as I walk through the doorway, my face falls.

Neil is sitting in front of my sister's missing poster on a flimsy metal chair and talking to my mother. She has her arm draped around his shoulder and he is holding a small cup of coffee that looks like it's about to crumble and spill everywhere all over his legs.

He's crying in big powerful sobs. They come into his body like a gust of wind and then are expelled just as quickly. Luke and I stand in the doorway. I take a quick look around to see if anyone is there and somehow, everyone has gone.

No deputies, no captain, there aren't even any volunteers. It's just my mom and Neil alone in the far corner of the room near the makeshift stage and the velvet curtains, as if they're in some sort of two person play with no audience.

I take a few steps. I lift my foot to take a step forward, but Luke stops me. It's almost as if he's reading my mind.

I glance over at him and he shakes his head.

"Why?" I mouth.

"It's not a good idea," he says without using words and just his face.

"Why?" I mouth again.

"They're having a moment," he says in a barely audible whisper. "He's telling her something. If you interfere right now, he may clam up and never tell us the truth."

I can't believe that I have to force myself to be quiet, to stand here and wait for my mother of all people to get some information from the person who might be the last one to have seen Natalie alive, but I know that Luke is right.

I know that this is the best thing to do.

I have no proof besides maybe just the hunch that Neil is involved at all. His parents have been acting overly protective and shady, but that doesn't mean that he's guilty.

He comes from a wealthy family and his father is a prosecutor, meaning that he knows exactly how this game is played and what some of the things are that his son should and should not say to law enforcement.

I take a step back to shift my weight and suddenly the floorboard creaks and both Neil and my mom snap to attention. My heart jumps into my chest and I don't dare take a moment to breathe. Instead, I examine his face. There're tears. It's wet, splotchy like he's been crying.

"Honey, come over here," Mom says, waving her hand in my direction.

I glance over at Luke who furrows his brow, neither of us expected this. I walk all the way across the room keenly aware of the three of them watching me. This is probably what it feels like to walk as a model on a catwalk, only I'm so much less graceful. My arms fall uncomfortably to my sides. I feel myself slouching and I straighten up my posture. My walk is interminable and I can't get there fast enough.

Mom introduces us and Neil says that we have already met.

"Will you please tell my daughter what you just told me?" she asks, still letting her arm droop off his shoulder but then grabbing on to his hand and giving it a squeeze for support.

"What is it, Neil?" I ask in my most non-authoritative voice possible. I want him to think of me as a friend, someone that he could share anything with, like apparently he did with my mom.

"I wanted to come here and talk to your mom in person, without my parents, lawyer, or other cops. She told me that you don't have jurisdiction here so you're not officially on the case."

"Yes, that's true," I say, clearing my throat, somewhat annoyed at my mom for going this far in divulging my employment status.

"I thought that she should know that we had plans to meet up that night, just me and Violet together."

"You did?" Luke approaches, but doesn't introduce himself and stands a little bit away from us. Just within earshot.

"We made plans for me to just pick her up right when Kaylee's mom dropped her off."

"Okay. So, what happened? Where did you go?" I ask.

I kneel down sitting on the back of my heels because I want to be on his level, but the nearest chair is a mile away on the other side of the room.

I'm tempted to ask Luke to grab me one, but I don't want him to miss a word of what Neil says for corroboration purposes.

"We just went and drove around," he says.

"That's it? For how long?"

"Like forty-five minutes. I was already there when Kaylee's mom showed up and I saw her leave the car. I was parked a little bit down the street, so I flagged her down before she went inside."

"Why didn't she just call my mom and tell her that she'd be late?" I ask.

"We weren't allowed to see each other," he says, looking straight at my mom and she nods to confirm this fact. Violet wasn't allowed to be out with boys.

"How did you get to the house?" I ask. "I mean, you don't drive?"

His cheeks start to burn and I can't tell if he is flushed with embarrassment, pity, or anger.

"I actually took my scooter over there. I'm not supposed to, I'm not even supposed to drive it on the roads, let alone at night, but it was going to take forever to bike over and she could get on the back of the scooter and we could go somewhere."

"So, what did you do exactly?"

"We drove around a little then ate some food."

"Did you stop somewhere?" I ask, immediately making a mental note to check the video cameras to confirm his story.

"No," he says. "I brought a couple of sandwiches from home, so we had a picnic out by the conservatory ... observatory," he corrects himself.

"You mean on the other side of the lake?"

"Yeah."

I know that there's a big park out there that's pretty popular with teenagers at night.

"So, you went out there and you just had a picnic?"

"Yeah."

"What happened then?"

"We hooked up."

"Did you have sex?"

My mom gasps and looks at me.

"Please ignore her. I have to know the truth. You're not in any trouble," I say, suddenly hating the fact that my mom is here making her judgements on someone who has to tell me everything.

"No, we didn't. We were taking it slow. We just made out and we were going to see each other again."

"Why didn't you tell me any of this before?"

"Natalie and I just got back together, but it wasn't working out, again. It was our fifth time and I was pressuring myself to give it a go. We've been together already for two years, so I figured I owe her that much."

I suddenly realize that he's barely thirteen, if that, fourteen and making plans for the rest of his life. I remember thinking this way when I was his age as well.

"So, you got back together with Natalie?"

"Yeah, just like the weekend before and then I saw Violet in school and I just had to be with her. I asked if she wanted to meet up and she said yes. I thought that she got an extension of her curfew or told you that she was still going to be with Kaylee. I just wanted to come and tell you, Mrs. Carr, in person that this is what happened and that I had nothing to do with her disappearance." He looks earnest and truthful, yet I don't know if I can believe him.

"So, what happened?" I ask. "I mean, how did you end things?"

"We stayed by the observatory for forty-five minutes and then she said she had to get back, so I dropped her back off and that's it. I never knew that she went anywhere else. I had no idea that she was even missing until the next day."

"What do you mean by went anywhere else?" I ask.

"Sorry, I just misspoke," he mumbles. "I mean, I had no idea that she was missing."

I nod and suddenly a group of volunteers comes to the door and I know that our conversation is over.

18

I glance over across the hall and see Captain Talarico walk in with a thick hoagie in his hand.

My face drops. Luke and I exchange a brief glance and we both know that we're about to catch hell for what happened here with Neil.

The captain has a jolly expression on his face, eager to dive into his lunch. He's holding a large, seventy-two-ounce gulp of soda in the other hand, wrapping his big sausage-y fingers around the top and sucking down on the straw. He waves to us.

I watch the way that the lines in his face strain out and the smile disappears when he sees Neil.

"What is he doing here?" he whispers, walking over to me in what seems to be two giant steps.

"I have to go," Neil says, "before my parents notice that I'm not home."

"Neil, I'm Captain Talarico," he says, extending his hand. "I'm the one in charge of looking for Violet and Natalie. I'd love to have a word with you."

"No, I can't," Neil says. "I really have to get back. I already told Mrs. Carr and the detective here everything that you need to know."

The captain is about to ask him again to stay, but Neil just brushes him off and walks out. The door slams and he turns toward us narrowing his eyes with anger.

"What the heck was that?" he snaps. "You interviewed a possible suspect or witness in this room right here without any recording equipment, without his parents?"

"This was not an interview," I say, throwing my hands up. "Not at all."

"It sounded like an interview."

"I didn't even know he was here."

My mom approaches.

"Captain, captain." She tries to cut in, but he continues to rant.

"I wasn't here," I insist.

"What about you?" he snaps at Luke. "Where were you?"

"We went and got lunch together," Luke explains in his most professional tone of voice. "She caught me up on the case."

"Oh, yeah. I bet."

"What is that supposed to mean?" I snap. "Are you trying to say that I did something improper?"

"Yeah. You interviewed Neil Goss without me or any of my deputies present. You have no jurisdiction here, Detective Carr. I don't know how many times I have to remind you of that."

"No. I came here, and I saw him talking to my mom. He found her and he wanted to tell her something. That's all that happened."

"Tell her what?" Captain Talarico finally turns his attention to my mom, who folds her hands across her chest, proudly, and waits for him to actually request an answer. "What is it that he told you, ma'am?"

"He sought me out. He knew what I looked like, but we'd never met. He asked to speak just to me, and we sat right there in those two chairs. He told me that he and Violet were together that night, after she got dropped off by Kaylee and her mom. They'd made plans earlier in the day at school. He picked her up on his scooter and they went out."

"Where?"

"To the observatory. They had a picnic. He brought two sandwiches." I'm surprised by my mom's succinct explanation of the facts.

No elaborations, no emotional details. It's the way that they teach you in the academy.

It's something that I have always struggled with, without adding in additional details. Like the fact that he was sobbing and how that made me feel.

"He cried," Mom says. "He was really upset. Kaitlyn and Luke can corroborate that."

The captain doesn't seem particularly satisfied with my mom's answers, but he focuses his discontent on me and Luke, the other law enforcement officers in the room.

"Did you talk to him about the inconsistencies in his statements about where he was that night?"

"I only came in at the end of this conversation," I say. "I didn't get a chance. I wanted to."

"That's the thing, that's why we do this in the proper place and at the proper time," he says.

"This is why we have interrogation rooms with cameras."

"Yes, I know that. I'm aware of the concept, but he was talking to my mom here. He was offering up information that we didn't currently have and frankly I don't understand why you're so pissed off about it."

"I'm pissed off because you didn't ask him the right questions. You had this one chance. Now he, as a minor, is going to go back home, talk to his prosecutor father, clam up, and we're not going to be able to get at the truth. You know just as well as I do that there was an inconsistency between where Natalie said she was the night of Violet's disappearance and where Neil said he was. He said he was with Natalie on the night Violet disappeared."

"Yes, I do know that, but that doesn't mean that he was going to answer those questions tonight. He came here to talk to my mom and just my mom to tell her that he was with Violet. That's it. I think that he did that without his father knowing and without his father's permission because he snuck out on his scooter, came here, and was very eager to go back as soon as his mission was accomplished."

Captain Talarico makes some disapproving puff of a sound and crosses his arms demonstratively to shut me out. I know that he is annoyed, pissed off.

He's not in complete control and the one thing we as law enforcement people hate is lack of control.

What else is there to do? I take a few steps away from him and he does the same thing. It's the only way to defuse the situation.

He needs space. He needs to regroup. If I keep pressing him and if we keep having this fight, then he's just going to dig in his heels and we're going to accomplish nothing.

19

I slip outside and decide that this is as good a time as any to try to find Violet's English teacher. I haven't brought up the fact that she might be lying on her grades to my mom yet and a part of me wonders if maybe she knows already but just didn't want to say anything. It would be better to have a few more facts available.

Much to my surprise, I find Miss Dolores in the parking lot talking to the two other teachers that I met during the search. She couldn't come to participate, but she wanted to be here to show her support. We shake hands and I pull her aside, not wanting anyone to influence her answers.

"Thanks for taking the time to talk to me," I say, as she wrings her hands nervously in front of me.

Her hair cascades down her shoulders in soft auburn waves and she has milky white skin with a few freckles, just on the bridge of her nose.

"Violet was a student of mine. I just can't believe that this happened to her, or to Natalie either."

"Can you tell me what your experience of Violet was? How is she as a student? What did you teach her?"

"Well, I had her for two years, last year for English A and then this year for English B."

"Okay. How was she?"

"Well, frankly, it's been like night and day."

"What do you mean?" I ask, pulling the small notebook out of my pocket. I hesitate but decide to ask if I can record her instead.

"I don't know."

"It's just for my own personal note taking, just to keep track of everyone's story. I just want you to please feel free to say anything because we just never know when some little insignificant detail is going to break this whole thing wide open."

I press record and she nervously shifts her weight from one foot to the other. Finally, she opens her mouth and starts talking.

"Violet is such a wonderful kid. Last year she would turn in all of her assignments on time. She would come and bug me and ask me incessant questions if she ever got anything lower than a B. When I saw that I had her in my class again, I was excited. I knew that she would bring everyone's general attitude up and she wouldn't be one of those kids complaining about too much work or too many projects. Morale is very important in middle school."

"Yes, I know," I say, briefly remembering my own time and all of the black I wore, paired with a black lipstick and all the cynicism I spewed about how love doesn't exist.

I was one of those kids who was always too cool for school. So, if there were anyone talking about their lives, anything emotional, or anything real, I went back to my sarcasm and my cynical analysis of how everything was stupid and not worth your time. "I'm glad that Violet was a good student. I'm glad that you enjoyed having her in your class."

"Yes, more than that, but it doesn't change the fact that recently, this past quarter something was off."

"What do you mean exactly?" I glance down at the recorder to make sure that it's getting it all down.

"She changed."

"Did she start to dress differently?"

"No, actually she didn't. She wore the same kind of bright sunny clothes she always had, but her attitude changed. She forgot a few big assignments and she told me that she was distracted, and I was stupid enough to believe her. The truth was that she didn't forget them, she didn't even do them at all. She didn't do them on purpose."

"How do you know?"

"I overheard her in the bathroom was talking to Carrie-Ann, this girl who is in eighth grade and she's not good news, Detective Carr."

"What do you mean?"

"She's always smoking in the bathrooms. When the dogs went around and smelled for drugs, her locker seemed to point to the fact that there was some evidence that there was marijuana in her locker. When we opened it there wasn't any, so we couldn't follow our zero-tolerance policy and expel her. She's a troublemaker. She talks back in class, she rarely does homework, and she's always skirting the rule about the length of her skirts. She got sent home a few times for wearing a midriff shirt."

"Wow, do they still have those rules?" I ask with a smirk on my face.

"Listen, I know that kind of policing of women's bodies is total crap. Okay? I realize that because boys can get away with wearing whatever, but those are the policies put in by the superintendent and we have to follow them. I let most people get away with a lot, but not bra tops, you know."

I nod.

"They're distracting. She knows that and she does it on purpose."

"Carrie-Ann. What is her last name?"

"Lebowski," Miss Dolores says.

I write down the name in my notebook.

"I had no idea that they were friends, but I guess they have been for a while now," she says. "I just happened to be in the bathroom when I heard them talking about it. I was in the stall and they didn't check underneath. They were just running their mouths about everything and everyone. I've never seen Violet like that before. She was just so confident and nonchalant. I mean, it was, on one hand, nice to see but on the other hand, very disturbing. She talked about how she didn't care about school anymore and she cursed a lot. She called me the 'B' word and then corrected herself and called me the 'C' word for giving her a D for an assignment she never turned in. It was disturbing and the thing is that I've never seen the two of them hang out together. Carrie-Ann is not known to have a lot of friends. She likes to push buttons and she likes to do what she likes to do."

"So, she's not in the same clique with Natalie and Neil?"

"No, not at all. Those kids know how to use soft power."

"What do you mean by that?" I ask. "You mean like in government?"

"You work in a school long enough and you realize that it's all about power dynamics. Middle school is brutal. Middle school is all about who you can step on to move up the rungs of popularity. People say that about high schools, but I think that in middle school you first realize the power that you can have over others and you don't have the empathy of high school students which should tell you a lot."

Her blue eyes narrow and the intensity in her face grows. She leans toward me and I no longer feel the nervous energy that used to emanate from her, instead something is different.

There's a kind of certainty that I haven't seen earlier.

"So, tell me more about Natalie and Neil," I press her.

"They're the popular kids at school. They, and her two brothers, are his best friends. He plays hockey and basketball. She's got about five other friends and he's got about four or five other friends. They rule the school. In terms of fashion, in terms of musical tastes, and in terms of everything. There're lots of kids that ignore them or basically don't even get on their periphery and Violet used to be like that."

"What about Carrie-Ann?"

"Carrie-Ann is an odd duck. She's like a jester. She sits in the back of class, makes fun of assignments, and mocks people under her breath when all of us teachers know exactly what she's saying, but we can't exactly draw more attention to it. She's not part of that clique, they're all pretty well off and their families go skiing together. Not here at Big Bear, in Colorado."

"So, how does Violet fit in?" I ask.

"Violet used to be kind of a wallflower. She was friends with Kaylee. She had a few other random friends who weren't friends with each other and she'd kind of sit and have lunch with whoever was available. I don't know exactly what happened. A few months ago, I saw her talking to Natalie and they were friendly. I was surprised. They might've worked on a project together in another class and then I saw her talking to Neil. I was like, wow, I guess they're taking Violet in and she's going to be part of the cool clique now, but, then there was Carrie-Ann. I know for sure that Natalie and Carrie-Ann never got along."

"Really, how?"

"They got into a fight in gym class, started screaming at each other. It almost got physical, but someone pulled them apart before that happened."

"Oh, wow," I mumble.

"Anyway, I don't know how they fit in with each other, but she was friends with both or at least it appeared to be that way."

"What about her grades? What happened there?"

"They started falling. She'd gotten mostly As before, but this past quarter she stopped turning in work. She would just not participate. She acted like she was better than everyone. So, I don't know if that was Carrie-Ann's influence or just her changing."

"Do you think something happened to cause that?"

"Yeah, something must have. For every action, there's an equal and opposite reaction, right?"

"I thought that you were an English teacher. That sounds like Physics to me." My joke lands, but she barely breaks a smile.

"I don't know what to do to help you, Detective," she says. "This is all I know. I'll talk to some more of my friends. I'll see what gossip I can dig up, but that's how it is. That's all I know."

I nod and thank her for her time. I give her my card and she gives me her phone number in case I need to follow up on anything. I walk away from her with a heavy heart. I appreciate everything that she has told me, but I suddenly realize just how much of a layered existence we all live, especially when we're in middle school. There are all these secrets and hidden truths. Of course, this is nothing that you would ever tell my mom. Maybe if I stayed here and we actually stayed in touch I might hear about ten percent of it.

This is what life is like at that age. You have friends, you try to make friends with others, you get lost, and you get confused. Someone may say one thing to you, then suddenly you stop being the person that you used to be, you become someone else entirely or maybe it's worse than that. Maybe it's not a word or a sentence that someone says, maybe it's something that someone did. Miss Dolores doesn't know anything about Violet and Neil except that they were friendly, but I know more. He wouldn't have been that upset and that distraught; he wouldn't be talking to my mom with tears in his eyes about spending an hour with her right before she disappeared, if he didn't care, if there weren't other secrets eating him up inside.

How do I figure all of this out? Where do we stand? I have to find out how Carrie-Ann is connected to all of this. I have to find out what else Neil didn't tell us about.

The truth is that this is what it's like to talk to suspects. They admit a little bit of the truth at a time. It's like admitting everything is too painful, but it's easier to get them to say that something was an accident first before circling back and calling them on the fact that it could never have been an accident.

I wonder what else Neil is hiding. He admitted that they were together, but what if that part where he dropped her off was a lie? What if he tried to go further, she said no, he did it anyway, and then he freaked out thinking that she was going to tell the police and he killed her? That sounds so mundane but that happens all the time. It's the stupidest reason, besides probably a car accident, to lose a life, but I've been doing this job long enough to know that it is often the cliché that takes us out in the end.

Luke catches up with me just as I'm wandering around the parking lot trying to process everything that Miss Dolores told me.

This all has to go in a report to be simplified and organized, yet it's in this period of transition where I don't know exactly what her words mean or imply.

This is where the world seems to make more sense, in this uncertainty.

Someone set up a makeshift coffee stand right next to the VFW, giving us a place to buy fresh roasted coffee without getting into our cars and driving to Starbucks. Luke buys me an espresso and I take it down in one gulp and then ask for a latte.

"Sorry about that," I say. "Just needed a little bit of a jolt of adrenaline. I feel myself drifting away from too little sleep."

20

A few hours later, Luke and I decide to get some takeout and eat at his hotel. It's the only place that we can be alone without drawing attention to ourselves and there's a great Nepalese restaurant in town, one of my favorites. I make suggestions for what is the best thing to order. We pick up the food and dig in feverishly sitting across from one another at the little table in his room. We don't say anything for a while until we're both done with about half of our cartons.

"Tell me about Violet," he says, chewing a little bit of food.

"What do you want to know?"

"Just what she's like."

"She's a good sister. We have such a big age gap that it feels almost strange. We had more of a mother-daughter relationship." It's hard for me to think back to what she was like as a kid without my eyes tearing up. Every day that passes there's more and more of a gulf that builds between us. "I don't want to talk about this," I say, looking away from him.

There's one light fixture above our heads with rounded edges and a delicate glass design reminiscent of the '70s. I stare at it because the light that emanates is low, like candlelight.

I don't know what I was expecting coming here. I guess another roll in the hay to take my mind off everything that's messed up in my life, but now suddenly, I feel myself getting closer to him and I'm not ready for that. Not in the least.

"What do you make of Neil?" I ask. "His whole thing, coming over to my mom. Do you think he was telling the truth?"

"Yeah, I do," Luke says, shifting his jaw from one side to the other.

"What do you mean?" I gasp.

"Just got that feeling, you know?"

I tilt my head and prop my chin up with my hand. I glare at him in disbelief.

"No, you can't be serious."

"I'm totally serious."

"What are you talking about? That's not...there's no way."

"What do you think? He just sought her out to place himself at the scene for no reason?" Luke asks, folding his arms across his chest.

"I have no idea what his motivation is, but he knows something. He was with her that night."

"Yes."

"The fact is that we would not know it if not for him coming forward and telling your mom about it. Remember, he did it secretly. He didn't tell the cops. He didn't tell his father. He came here on a scooter because he doesn't drive."

"So, just because he doesn't drive means that he can't be responsible for someone's death?" The words just spill out of me.

"What are you talking about?"

Suddenly, everything goes black.

"I haven't let myself think that thought before. Dead, death. Deceased, departed. There're so many euphemisms and metaphors. There's a finality to it that doesn't come with the word gone."

"You think that she's dead? You of all people?" Luke asks. "Please tell me you don't."

"I don't know what to think," I say. "My sister's missing for days. She's disappeared. Nothing about my life makes any sense right now. Realistically speaking, she may be dead."

"Don't say that." Luke throws his hand in my face. "You know that there is a strong possibility that she's alive. She's not a small child. She's a teenager."

"You think she ran away?"

"No, I'm not saying that, but if someone took her there's a strong possibility they're keeping her alive."

That phrasing, his word, sends a shiver through my body. They're keeping her alive and doing what, the worst possible things that men tend to do to women or little girls.

"Do you want her to be dead? Is that easier for you?"

"Shut up," I say, getting up from my seat and resisting the urge to slap him across the face. "How dare you say that? Of course, I don't want her dead. I'm just..."

"You're being a realist? I don't think so." Luke shakes his head. He remains seated but turns his body toward mine as I pace in front of the television.

Suddenly, the small motel room feels even tighter and more cramped as the walls start to close in around me.

"I want to leave, but this conversation isn't over. There's still so much more to say."

"Tell me why Neil would kill her or hurt her?" Luke challenges me.

"It's a story as old as time. He tries to take it a little further with her and she's not happy with it, but he keeps doing it. Maybe he fondles her, maybe he rapes her, and then he feels bad. He starts to think, 'What's going to happen when I drop her back off at home? Is she going to call the police? Is my life going to be over?' So, he picks up a rock and he hits her on the head. He buries the body somewhere."

"Where? At the observatory?" He asks.

I clench my jaw.

"Highly unlikely, because we've never looked there and he would be pointing us in that direction, but yeah, he buries her somewhere."

"How does he get her there?" He asks.

"What are you talking about?"

"How does he physically take her from that park near the observatory to this other place? He has only a scooter, remember? So, does he drape her body over it?"

"I don't know, but we have to look there."

"Deputies are already doing that, remember?" he says, reminding me of what the captain mentioned offhandedly.

"I have to go and look there, too," I say.

"You're not going to be able to find anything tonight unless it's the body and I'm sure that the sheriff's deputies can do that very well without you, but the thing is, Kaitlyn, that this doesn't make sense. We were never looking for her in that spot. So, why would he come here and confess this thing to your mom, unless everything he said was true? He was there. They did have a picnic. Then he dropped her back off. That's it. End of story."

I pace from one side of the room to another processing what he is saying. My blood pressure is elevated. I feel tense and nothing seems to make sense, except that something keeps gnawing at me.

"You know as well as I do that people tend to come forward with only a part of the story. They tell a million half-truths and you have to keep interviewing them to get the rest of it. They're not going to come right out and admit that what they did is rape and kill this girl. He's going to say something else, he's going to place himself at the scene because he's worried that we're going to find some evidence of him being there anyway. He's just going to preemptively explain it away. We have to keep digging and keep getting more information in order to find out what happened."

"Listen, if you want to think that, that's fine, but I'm going to wait for the sheriff's department to do their search and see if they do actually find any evidence of them being there, let alone a murder taking place."

I slow down my pacing back and forth and take a few deep breaths to calm down. I sit on the edge of the bed.

"There's something else," he says. "Natalie."

I nod.

"She's still missing. If you think this kid killed Violet or had anything to do with her disappearance, then you probably think he has something to do with Natalie's disappearance. What are the chances of a thirteen-year-old making two of his friends disappear? Doesn't that sound like a job for an adult?"

I nod. I know what he's saying is right.

"What if he was involved?" I ask.

"Yeah. He may be involved and I'm not saying that he's not capable of it. I am. I know that plenty of thirteen year olds have committed murder and many more will continue to do so, but the thing is that they're both missing. We found nothing, no evidence, no fingerprints at either scene, no camera presence from the neighbors' Nest cameras, no witnesses, no sign that they were abducted, let alone killed."

"What does that tell you?"

"If Neil is involved, he's involved with somebody else."

"So, what do you think happened?" I ask. "You think that it was some shadowy figure driving around grabbing girls from their porches?"

"Yeah, that's possible, but again, we don't have any strange cars on cameras recorded in the neighborhoods. The canvassing didn't result in a single lead about a stranger being there. It's a mystery and until we get more information, it's going to remain a mystery."

I swallow hard. I wanted to keep this information to myself, but now I realize that I can't.

"There's something else," I say. "Captain showed me her computer. She had all these videos of them making out, having sex."

"Yes, I know." He nods his head.

"You know?"

"They turned over all of their files to me and my team. I watched the videos. Violet is there in the basement recording them and they're very well aware of the fact that she's there. It is not a hidden camera."

"Why though?"

"I don't know. I don't know why teenagers record and make pictures of half the things that they do, but whatever they were doing, it was at least consensual from what I can tell from the video footage."

"Don't you think that gives Neil some sort of motive?"

"Yeah. If anything, it gives Natalie motive because of how society is. A boy gets with a hot girl and he's made out to be some charismatic Casanova. If a girl does it, then she's damaged goods. There's nothing on any of those videos that seems like he or they are doing anything without their consent. Even if Neil didn't want those videos to get out, there's no evidence that Violet was planning on releasing them. She, in fact, is the one who's the creepy one in the videos, standing there and recording everything."

"There's one with her and Neil, too," I say.

"There is." He nods. "I saw that. It's still not clear how any of this is related to their disappearance. We're going to have our computer techs work on it. Maybe they were uploaded somewhere to some site. Maybe that will lead us and give us some clues, but so far, it seems like all the evidence is pointing to a stranger taking them or..." His voice drops off.

"Or what?" I ask.

"Or them going somewhere on their own."

"No," I shake my head, "absolutely not."

"I know that you think it's unlikely, but you also know that Violet has had a secret life, and that doesn't mean that there aren't more secrets to uncover."

21

I get a call from Captain Medvil and I immediately answer to find out that Robert Kaslar is coming in to speak to them without a lawyer at eight a.m. the following morning.

Medvil is brief and he gets to the point right away.

"Can I come? Will I be there to do the interview?" I hesitate briefly and he senses that.

He says, "I can assign someone else to this case, Kaitlyn, you know that?"

"I know," I say, "but this is my case and I've done all the other interviews, so I need to do this one."

"Okay, but only if you're here on your own time and you're fully committed, because I just can't have this going back and forth, you know?" he asks.

I nod.

"Carr?" he asks, and I suddenly remember that he can't see me.

"I'll be there. The investigation here has kind of reached a bit of a pause. So, I'll be there, and I'll do the interview 100% committed, sir."

He hangs up without a goodbye. I exhale slowly.

I know that this is the right thing to do. I've already gotten a lot out of him and I think that, in a different environment, with cameras and a little bit of pressure, I can push him over the edge and get him to tell me what he did to his wife.

"So, you're going back?" Luke asks.

I nod and answer, "I can't let him re-assign this case. Robert already told me a lot, and I think he's kind of afraid of me. I probably have the best chance of getting him to open up."

"Hey, you don't have to explain it to me."

"Besides, if I get re-assigned then I may catch a murder investigation and you know how those are.

There's the additional pressure from the forty-eight-hour time clock so everything's accelerated."

"Listen, I know exactly what you do, and what you need to do. I get it," Luke says, but I sense a pulling away from him. I know that he doesn't want me to leave, at least that's what it feels like.

"I want to apologize for the argument that we had earlier, but the problem is that I'm not sorry. It's good that we disagreed. It's good to have opposing opinions just in case things don't go as planned."

"Listen, I have to tell you something," Luke says, sitting down next to me on the edge of the bed. I grab the remote control, turn on the TV, and let it bathe us in a deep blue light. Luke reaches over and flips it off.

"What's wrong?" I ask.

"I don't know how to say this to you exactly because I wasn't expecting us to get together earlier, but I actually have a date tonight and I have to go." "What?"

His words sound jumbled and I'm not entirely sure if I understood what he's saying.

"What are you talking about? What do you mean you have a date? Who do you even know here?"

"It's not here. It's down in San Bernardino. My cousin lives in Riverside and she set up this double date with her and her boyfriend a while ago. I can't cancel. This is her friend and... I don't know. I just can't cancel. It's been set up for like a month, way before us."

"Okay." I nod.

"Nothing's going to happen. I mean, I like you."

"I like you, too, but, you know, this isn't serious or anything. You don't have to run anything past me," I say defensively.

Now it's his turn to look surprised. His eyebrows rise and he nods very slowly and suddenly I regret what I had said.

"Well, I just wanted...I just wanted to let you know, to be a nice guy, but I had no plans for it to be a real date, but my cousin..."

"Listen, you don't have to explain anything," I cut him off. "You have a date, fine. Whatever. We're just friends, right?"

"Well, I thought," he starts to say.

"If you thought that we're more than that, then why are you going on this date?"

"I told you, it was something that was set up earlier."

"Okay, well, then go. That's totally fine. You go on your date and I'm going to drive back and get some sleep before my interview tomorrow."

I start to head toward the door, but he grabs my hand.

"Listen, I told you, if you want to go, go," I snap.

His eyes dart from side to side but focus on mine. He's basically asking me to stop him, but I refuse to play that game. We're not together and if he doesn't want to go on this date, then he has to stop himself.

"Listen," I pull my hand away from him, "you don't owe me anything. You can go and do whatever you want."

He nods and bites the inside of his cheek. I want to take that back. I shouldn't have said that, but I grab my purse, zip up my jacket, and I walk out into the cold.

I FEEL LOST. I'm not certain of anything. I'm not certain of my own instincts or what feels like the right thing is. I knew that Luke and I weren't officially together, but I had no idea that he was making other plans, other dates. I know that he's not lying when he said that his cousin had set him up on this date before we even met and he's just going on it as an obligation.

I turn on the music and I turn it up really loud, to try to drown out my own thoughts. It works for a little while, but every time I come to a stop sign, to a light, or just a little bit of a traffic jam, my thoughts immediately return to him.

Was I a fool for acting like that? Did I make a mistake?

Did I push him away when he really wanted me to stay close? This wouldn't be the first time.

The history of my relationships is a battlefield of bad decisions. Yes, there have been a few that were unhappy with my working schedule, but those boyfriends have been sparse.

Most of the time, I can't commit. I can't put myself out there.

When someone asks, "Be mine, just mine. Let's try to make a life together," I'm afraid. I know that it probably goes back to my childhood and how uneven and unstable it was to be my mother's child.

Sometimes everything was fine, we were a happy family. Other times she'd come home from work and everything would be wrong, mismanaged, and just off.

My father didn't add to the general good feeling in the house. He would drink, he would do drugs, and he would disappear. Being with him was probably what made my mom so worried about the future and uncertain of the present.

Some days they'd kiss, hug, and watch a movie on the couch. Others he'd be gone, partying, selling drugs, just not spending time with us.

You never knew what you were going to get. For some people, that was probably a source of excitement, but not in my family.

It made my mom crave stability and it made me crave independence.

I would not be like her and my happiness would not depend on a man. It wouldn't matter if I had one or not. They can come and go.

I could have a good time, but I would have no connections. That has always been my motto. That's why I always ran.

Stability was just not worth the price that it required you to pay. My thoughts return to Luke.

Something is different about him. He's quiet, reserved, and unassuming. Other people wouldn't think that he's very fun, but I do. I kind of like that. He makes me laugh.

The world seems okay when he's around, but the minute that he told me that he had a date, a switch went off, and suddenly everything changed. Reflecting back on that moment in the motel, I realize that I tend to walk on thin ice.

The minute I see a crack I make a jump for it and run away, but that's not always right, right? A crack doesn't always mean that something is terribly, irrevocably wrong. Sometimes it's something that can be fixed.

When I get to my apartment and climb under the covers, I'm filled with nothing but regret for how I acted. He told me that he had a date and instead of talking to him, I ran away. I told him that it didn't matter that he had a date and that I'd be fine either way.

Now he's out there meeting this girl without problems, without baggage, someone who can love him for who he is, and I pushed him away. I pushed him into her arms and it's all my fault.

I sleep like a rock and I get to work early the next morning to go over all of my notes and prepare for the interview with Robert. Captain Medvil is happy to see me and offers to walk me through what we have on the case so far. It's not much, just a lot of suspicious talk and uncertainty.

"Frankly, we don't even know whether or not she's missing of her own volition," the captain says.

"Looking over the case file, we can assume that she isn't, given the fact that she's not using her phone or her laptop," I say.

"No, I don't think so." He shakes his head. "She could be running away from him. Maybe he was abusive and no one knew. Maybe she doesn't want to be found. Maybe she got a burner phone at Walmart with no registration with the phone company."

"That's plausible, I guess," I say, "but what about her friend? What about her doctor's appointment? Why would she just disappear right after the trip? Why wouldn't she at least tell her friend not to worry?"

"I guess that's what we have to find out from Robert."

"No, I don't have a good feeling about this," I say. "I think that if she's gone, she's not gone of her own volition."

We sit with that for a few minutes around his desk with neither of us saying anything and both of us burying our eyes in the case file even though what we look at is nothing in particular.

"What about her parents? Also, were you able to get anyone in the media interested in this case?"

"That's the thing," I say. "Her parents are across the country in South Carolina. So, the local stations ran a few reports about her being missing but there's no one to interview. There's no one locally besides her friend to participate in the search. So, they're having trouble gaining interest in her story."

He looks at a recent picture of Karen, smiley face, tousled hair, and features that aren't exactly selling a lot of newspapers. Neither of us wants to say it but we know why the media isn't interested.

She didn't have much of an online presence and she didn't have many friends. She also doesn't have family members to interview and cry in front of reporters. There isn't any concrete evidence or even enough to make an accusation against her husband.

"I mean, she is pregnant," I say. "They always like the stories about pregnant women."

"Yeah, that's true. Has that been confirmed?"

"We need a warrant to access her medical records, otherwise the gynecologist won't tell me anything. Just between you and me, she did give me a wink, so to speak, but she won't go public with it."

"Well, she did take all of those pregnancy tests that she told Elin about, right?" the captain asks.

I nod.

He takes a long sip from his canister, undoubtedly filled with the darkest, blackest coffee imaginable.

"So, what do you want me to ask him?" I ask Captain Medvil. "Anything specifically to focus on?"

"You know what to do," he says confidently. "You're good at this."

I nod. I've been having doubts and I appreciate him saying this.

"Just press what you know about from Elin and the doctor. Push him to say anything about seeing her even a little bit, even for a short time after she got back from her business trip. Maybe he made a mistake. Maybe they had a fight and he didn't mean for anything to happen."

That's the usual technique when it comes to these interrogations. First, you get the person to admit that they were there. Then you get them to say that whatever happened was an accident.

People are more likely to admit to an accident than doing it on purpose. Once you have that on record and on file, you press harder. You show them all the ways that it could never have been an accident. That's when the confession usually occurs. They try to prove you wrong. They talk themselves into a corner. They admit to more things that happened to try to show you that they are right and that's when they get in trouble. That's how they slip up.

My only purpose here is to get Robert to do this, to get him to tell us what happened to Karen, and what he did to her. I have one chance at this, technically, more than that. There're infinite chances, but people get frustrated when you ask them the same questions and they either give you the same answers or they clam up entirely.

No, with him I have to show myself to be just the right type of person, the kind of person that he would open up to.

I have to challenge him, but not so much that it forces him to shut down.

I have to be his friend, but not a pushover.

It's a fine line to walk.

22

I walk into the interrogation room with my hair pinned neatly to the nape of my neck. I'm dressed in a suit, a pencil skirt, and I have a black faux leather, shoulder bag, out of which I pull out his case file.

I just touched up my makeup a few minutes before, added a little bit of red lipstick and another bit to my lashes. I want to look friendly, young, and inviting, but serious as well.

I know that if he's getting away with doing something to his wife, he must think that I'm a fool, inexperienced, someone who will never get to the bottom of what's going on. I have that to my advantage. Now, I just have to use it.

"Thank you for coming in, Mr. Kaslar."

"Robert, please," he says.

We shake hands and I point to the sturdy metal chair with a straight back for him to sit in.

I arrive right on time and don't make him wait long. I may use time to my advantage later on when I want him to think about something that I reveal in the interrogation, but for now, I don't want to make him wait. I want to show him that I appreciate him taking the time to meet with me.

"I have to be at work at nine, ten at the latest."

"Okay. Then we'll be brief."

There's a cup of coffee in front of him, which I'm certain the deputy brought in. It has the same familiar branding on the front, moose and the antlers from the local coffee shop just around the corner.

It's much better than the kind that the assistants and the front desk people make here in the department usually reserved for special and honorary guests like Robert.

I open the file demonstratively in front of him, even though I have memorized every detail in it. I want him to see how big it is and to acknowledge the fact that his wife is actually missing, and we are actually investigating it.

Unlike back at his house, Robert doesn't appear to be nervous. He's not wearing a beanie on his head. His hair is freshly washed and so is his face. He's wearing a button-down shirt with an unwrinkled collar, something that he either ironed or had taken a lot of effort in keeping unwrinkled. The shirt has a checkered pattern of blue and white and he's wearing a pair of khakis, the uniform of a computer scientist.

"So, what do you want to ask me?" he asks, folding his hands in front of me and looking straight into my eyes.

I wonder where all of this confidence is suddenly coming from.

Does he know something that we don't? Is he certain that we will never find out?

"I want to go over your testimony again about how your wife went missing."

"Yeah, sure. If you want to waste more time," he says nonchalantly, but keeping his gaze straight on me.

"You think it's a waste of time?"

"Yes. I think it's an insane waste of time. I told you everything that I know." Suddenly, he is fired up, irritated, on edge, and the way it happened, it was like a light switch. One minute calm, the next, pissed off.

"There are certain inconsistencies."

"Like what?" he snaps.

"Like the fact that you said you weren't aware of the fact that your wife was pregnant. Your wife was, let's say, obsessed with having a child, but you?"

"I already told you I didn't really want to, but if she wanted to, that was fine by me."

"Despite the fact that you just had a baby with your girlfriend?"

"I don't want to talk about that." He clenches his jaw. "I'm here to talk about my wife. My personal life has nothing to do with this."

"Actually, I would disagree with that statement, wholeheartedly."

"I don't care," he snaps again. His nostrils flare and his eyes narrow.

I wait for him to make a move to say something else, but he seems to calm himself down. "Look,

my wife found out I was having an affair. Big deal.
Our relationship was off the rails way before that
happened, okay? She said she wanted to have a
baby. Well, we never had sex. Like once every two,
three months if I was lucky. You don't do that if
you want to have a baby, right? My wife had a lot
of issues. She wanted to do IVF, okay?"

"So, you knew about that?"

"Yes."

"You didn't mention that before," I point out. "I
don't know what you know, Robert, please. I just
need you to tell me as much as you can. It'll be
easier for both of us during this process."

"I'm sorry that I lied about the affair," he says
after a long pause. "It was stupid. I shouldn't have
done it."

"The affair or the lie?"

He hesitates but says, "Both, but that has nothing
to do with my wife's disappearance, okay? I had
nothing to do with it. I wasn't there when she
came home from her business trip. You know that.
You must have gotten some sort of footage from
the neighbors, right?"

I nod but reveal nothing.

"What about the cameras on the back? You said that there were cameras. Did you see her leave? Did you get any details about what might have happened or are you still processing those?"

Suddenly caught off guard by his question I respond, "The truth is that there are no cameras to process." So, therefore, I have no idea if she ever went out that way or if he ever took her out that way.

"Well, whatever. I don't know what happened. Elin was the last person to see her. She said that she came into the house. So, I guess that's what happened. I was working late. She wasn't here. I didn't get home until the morning. So, I don't know what you expect me to know, but I don't know a thing."

I inhale slowly and exhale even slower. He's very good at this. The guy that I met at his apartment was sketchy, out of control, and shy.

Now he seems like a completely different person. Is it because we're recording the session?

Is it because he wants to appear like an outraged husband?

Is it because he actually has no idea where his wife went?

"What do you think happened?" I ask, folding my hands in front of him and intertwining my fingers. "We're out of ideas."

"Already? You're the LAPD, how can you be out of ideas?"

"We've interviewed, simple as that. We interviewed her friends, canvassed the neighborhood, talked to your neighbors. She's gone. So, unless you give us something to go on or someone to talk to."

"What about her parents? What did her parents say?" he asks.

"Why don't you tell me?" I say.

"They have no idea. They live in South Carolina," he barks. A little droplet of spit lands on my cheek and I wipe it off and glare at him.

"I'd appreciate it if you didn't spit on me," I say.

"Listen, I'm just upset," he says, leaning over the table.

It takes all of my strength not to pull away from him and remain exactly where I am despite the fact that he's invading my personal space. "I don't know where my wife is, okay? I want you to find her. I didn't tell you about my affair because we all know that it looks bad. She caught me. I have a child. I want to leave her, okay? I was going to leave her."

"What if she was pregnant?"

"I don't know. It'd be a miracle if she were. So what?"

"So what? He or she'll be your baby."

"Yeah, but I don't want to be with her anymore. I want to be with my girlfriend and my baby. So, if the paternity test says that the baby's mine, then I'll accept the child as my own. Pay child support, do visitation, whatever."

This catches me by surprise, but I decide to just go with it.

"Let's go back to her parents. They don't like you very much, do they?"

"Yeah. They don't. They never have."

"They mentioned that you haven't visited them for the last few Christmases," I point out, quoting verbatim from the interview that another detective had conducted with them.

"Yeah. So what? I don't have much time off and I didn't want to waste it flying over there and spending time with people I don't like. She went by herself."

"They seem pretty convinced that you have something to do with their daughter's disappearance."

"Listen, Danila and Brad have hated me for years, okay? They never wanted us to get married. They never wanted to get to know me. They always tried to poison our relationship. I was putting up with it, but I wasn't going to make any extra effort. Not on her behalf anyway."

"Why? She's your wife."

"Every time she would talk to her mom, we'd get into a huge fight, okay? Her mom was pressuring her to have children way before she was ready. Making her feel bad about how old she is and how everyone her age has children. All of that crap that women think. In reality, my wife, she didn't want to have kids at all, not for years. That was fine with me. We would have been happily married for many years if her parents hadn't gotten themselves so involved in our lives." He sits back in the chair and takes a few big gulps of his coffee.

I regroup. I look through the file to try to think of a different way to approach this conversation. He has revealed some additional clues, but we're nowhere near to getting to the real answers.

"Listen, I have to go," he says, looking at his watch.

"We're not through with this conversation," I say.

"That may be the case, but I am, okay? I came in here. I talked to you on three separate occasions. I think that's enough."

"It's not, I have a lot of things to still discuss with you."

"I'm tired of going in circles, okay? You don't seem to understand. I had nothing to do with my wife's disappearance and the more time that you focus on me, the less time that she has."

I listen for past tense and I listen for any clues as to the fact that he might think that she's no longer here, but I don't hear anything.

"I would like you to stay longer, please. I'll get right to the point. I have a few more questions."

"I can't. I told you how much time I had."

"This isn't a request," I say, getting desperate.

"Yes, it is." He stands up. "Unless you are putting me under arrest. You're asking me to stay and I'm not missing work because of this crap." He stands up and walks to the door. He waits for me to stop him, but he and I both know that I can't.

"Next time you want to talk to me, you call my lawyer," he says, putting the metaphorical nail in the coffin.

He walks out of the interrogation room and I see the case slipping between my fingers.

23

After a somewhat disastrous interview, I lick my wounds over lunch. Early lunch, it's barely eleven, but my stomach is growling since I haven't had anything substantial to eat since the night before. Much to my surprise, my phone goes off. When I look down at the screen, I see that it's Mark.

I had programmed his phone number from his card into my phone just in case he ever called without really expecting him to. I'm tempted to let it go to voice mail, but then I click accept.

He invites me out for drinks after work for happy hour. I know that I should go back to Big Bear, but all of the driving is wearing me down. I need a break. Just someone who doesn't work in law enforcement. I need to talk about something different, be with someone different.

When he asks me out, I just say yes. I have a whole afternoon until our meeting, so I decide to drive up to Reseda to talk to Robert's girlfriend. I don't know if I'm going to get any answers, but she's the one person I haven't spoken to yet. I wonder what details she can shed on this whole situation.

I check in with Captain Medvil and he approves the move, even though he's still upset with me for not getting through everything we needed to cover with Robert earlier. The thing about this job is that everything is in delicate balance. You really have only one, or at most a few opportunities to get a confession. In this case, we don't have a body. We don't even have much evidence that she didn't leave of her own free will. So, everything seems to be pinned on that elusive confession.

The general public thinks that confessions are either something that only guilty people admit to, but there's a long history in criminology of detectives getting innocent people to confess to crimes they didn't commit. It's easier and it's much more common than you think.

It starts with admitting that you were there. After hours of interrogation, maybe you could be there. Maybe you just forgot.

Once the suspect admits to that and places himself at the scene, then it's easier for you to nitpick and get him to confess to other things. I would go so far as to say that no detective wants a false confession, but that doesn't mean they don't want a confession.

In certain circumstances, you just believe that someone did something. You see through the evidence. Sometimes the evidence is meager, or light, and other times, there's just still not enough of it, no matter how much there is.

The confession seals the deal. It presents the case for the prosecutor on a silver platter, so to speak. All detectives want to close cases and solve crimes.

Zigzagging up the narrow Laurel Canyon road, I admire the houses perched on the cliff sides and their precarious existence, despite the mudslides and the rains that occasionally take one or two of them out every year.

This was always one of my dream places to live. Hollywood Hills is very similar, but this is the canyon that I always drive when I try to get to the valley. There're even a few houses that cost about

$5 million each that I can't help but dream about. I'll never own a house like that, not as long as I have this job. Wait, let me correct myself. Not as long as I am an honest cop.

When I first got started, the precinct by MacArthur Park in downtown LA got shut down. They actually had a sting operation with a few undercover cops taking down their coworkers, that entire precinct or, very nearly all of it, consisted of corrupt cops who dealt drugs and used their shields for protection to gangsters and the mob.

One of them actually had a house in the Hollywood Hills and another one. If you lived in Calabasas, all the property was registered in the names of their wives or children or close friends, but everyone knew what was going on, at least after the sting operation.

I get to Reseda in no time flat, due to hitting practically every green light and encountering very little traffic. The house is located on a little treelined street with cars parked out in front instead of in garages. This is an older area, and the houses have a historic craftsman quality to them, while others are just low-level construction popular in the '70s. Very few had garages at that time and very few were required to have attached garages.

I park in front of Margaret Layne's house and note the giant red rose bushes spilling over the white picket fence that's freshly painted and clearly loved. It looks like a lovely little house, in a picturesque little town, in a Hollywood movie, rather than in a bedroom community attached to so many others in Los Angeles.

There's no way to get to the front door except to open the gate. I walk through the rose garden and knock on the bright blue door. There's no doorbell, just an ornate brass knocker in the shape of an elephant.

There's a Subaru parked in the driveway and I know that she has a baby, who I really don't want to wake up. I knock again hoping that I'm not too loud but yet loud enough to get her attention.

Margaret answers the door with a big smile on her face and her hair tied up into a loose bun on the top of her head. She smiles widely at me and I notice the beads of sweat on her forehead and across her chest, like she has been exercising. Her face is flushed, but beautiful with delicate features and big almond eyes; she's slim and dressed in yoga pants and a matching sports bra.

I introduce myself and her face falls immediately. I ask her if I can come in to talk for a little bit. She hesitates and finally agrees.

She shows me inside her craftsman bungalow with wide white trim around the single pane windows and a matching trim around the fireplace and living room. Everything in the home looks well-loved and taken care of. There is a big tapestry above the sleek gray couch featuring an elephant as well as a few more elephant style décor items; elephant candlesticks, a lamp with the trunk of the elephant holding up the shade, and barely visible etchings of elephants on the curtains swinging in the wind.

"I just finished a yoga class," she says, pointing to the couch for me to sit down. There's no coffee table, just two end tables and I realize that this is probably because she has a small child who's just starting to walk.

"My baby is in the other room sleeping," she says quietly.

"Okay, good. This shouldn't take long. You were doing yoga?" I ask, wondering if someone was home babysitting the child while she was in class.

"Yeah. Online. I teach over Zoom," she says. "I have clients all over the US and some in Europe. I usually teach seven days a week, occasionally six." She wipes her brow with the back of her arm. "Sorry, I'm so sweaty," she says, getting up and grabbing a towel from her yoga setup in the other room.

There's a laptop on top of a chair angled down as well as blocks and a stretch band on either side of the teal green yoga mat. I'm not usually a fan of small talk, but it's easier to dive into more difficult conversation topics after a little bit of chitchat.

I ask a few more questions about her practice, and she tells me that she's been doing it for a few years after getting fired from a yoga studio due to a series of layoffs and consolidations of spaces.

"I figured this way I'd be in charge of all the income that I bring in. Sometimes, it's not as much as I used to make, especially in the beginning, but now I have a good group of clientele and it has really grown."

"Good. I'm glad that's working out," I say.

I pull out my notebook, signaling that we're about to get down to the nitty-gritty. I ask her about Robert, and she confirms that they've been seeing each other for close to two years.

"How did you meet?"

"Actually, at work. His company brought me in to do this meditation and yoga practice for the employees. We started chatting. He was a really funny guy. We had a lot in common. He likes horror movies and so do I. So, he asked me out."

I wonder if it would be odd for a yoga teacher, who is all into peace and tranquility, or at least should be, would be into horror movies, but I guess it's just as much of an interest as any other.

"So, did you know that he was married when you met?"

"No." She shakes her head.

"You didn't?"

"No, I would never go out with someone who's married."

"So, what happened?"

"I looked through his phone one day. I don't even remember why; it was like a message came in and he told me to give it to him or something like that, and that's when I saw her name and all their conversations. He was never really active on social media. He didn't list himself as married, nothing like that. So, I had no clue."

"What happened then?"

"I left him."

"You did?" I ask, surprised.

"Yeah, I did. Then two months later, I found out that I was pregnant, and I went to tell him that I was going to keep the baby. He started telling me all this stuff about how much he loved me and missed me and that he wanted to leave his wife to be with me. I was pregnant and emotional, and they didn't have any kids, so I believed him. I was so stupid."

"So, what happened when his wife showed up? She did show up here, right?"

"Yeah," she says after a long pause. "She did. He told me that they'd separated and that she'd moved out. We were spending a lot of time together, almost every evening. Sometimes he even left work early."

"So, he wasn't working late most nights?"

"No. He'd just come here right after work."

"Oh, okay."

"Then one night, about two weeks ago, she just showed up with her friend," she says. "We were in the pool out back and she started screaming at him. It was terrible. My neighbors heard everything. It was so embarrassing. I was so angry with him, and I was so angry with myself. I just couldn't believe that he would do something like that. In retrospect, he lied to me once, why wouldn't he lie to me again?"

"So, what happened that day, or after?"

"Her friend was there and she kind of pulled her away. They left eventually, but she was really belligerent. After that I told him to leave. I told him I didn't want to hear from him again. I didn't want anything to do with him."

"What about your child?"

"I told him that I wouldn't fight for visitation or anything like that, but he'd have to put in the effort and actually make arrangements. I was done taking care of everything in that relationship. I was so exhausted and tired of just being with him."

She puts her head down and buries her face in her knees and begins to sob. Big, sad sobs. The kind that makes it almost painful for you to hear. She chokes up a few times and it takes her a few minutes to gather her composure. Wiping her eyes, she looks up and apologizes.

"The thing about Robert is that he makes you feel like everything is perfect when you're together. Like finally your life makes sense and you've found a perfect partner, but then he hides all this stuff from you. He has all these secrets, and I never knew that he was keeping all these things from me. I guess he figured that I would never date him if I knew he was married, and I never would have, let alone have a child with him. I didn't want to break up a marriage, I hope that you believe that," she says, looking straight into my eyes.

"That was never my intention. And as soon as I found out that they were not in fact separated, I told him that we were over. I don't want to be with a liar. I want to be with someone I can trust, love, and care for. I don't want to share him with anyone."

She looks down at her ring finger and twists the tiny opal ring around a few times until the gemstone comes right back to the top.

"Do you think that's why he killed her?" Her words feel like they have knocked the wind out of me, and for a moment, I can't breathe in or out.

I lean forward and ask, "What do you mean?"

"She's gone. No one knows where she is."

"What did Robert tell you?"

"Nothing. I don't know anything, but his wife is gone and you're here asking questions about his affair and he had all these secrets."

"So, he never discussed or said anything about his wife maybe not being here anymore?"

"No. Absolutely not. I watch Oxygen and WE TV and I know how it works out for missing wives."

"How's that?"

"Not great. Most of the time it's the husband, right?"

"Can you show me any texts that you guys shared?" I ask. "Would you be okay with that?"

"Yes, you can see anything," she says nonchalantly. "We texted, but like I said, he wasn't really much on social media, so I could never tag him in any of my pictures."

"So, he didn't even have an account?"

"No. I guess I should have found that odd, but it was actually refreshing. I remembered how much I enjoyed the fact that not everything about his life was 100% public like it is with most people our age. I didn't have to worry about showing up on his Instagram account and have my ex-boyfriends look at that. I guess it's a sign that something's off, huh?"

Her baby starts to cry in another room, and she excuses herself, handing me her laptop and her phone. Her openness with her private accounts takes me by surprise because for half of this conversation, or maybe even 75% of it, I thought that she had something to do with Karen's disappearance.

I LOOK through Margaret's texts and scroll up as far as I can get in the conversations with Robert. There are no naked pictures and no inappropriate talk. Of course, they did spend a lot of time together in real life, since apparently he wasn't working late at all and that makes me wonder. That explains why there weren't that many sexually explicit messages. I couldn't even find one. I hear her talking to her daughter and singing to her and I realize that I have a little bit more time.

I look through her computer and check the Zoom and click on her calendar. On the night of the eighteenth, when Karen came back from her business trip, Margaret had yoga from nine until eleven at night, two separate sessions. I click over to the next day and see that she was basically booked with clients for seven hours that day, starting from eight in the morning, without even a break for lunch.

Just because these meetings were in her calendar, doesn't mean that she was there. Margaret comes back and sees the calendar open on my lap.

"I'm sorry. I hope this is okay," I say. "I just wanted to see what you had going on the night of her disappearance."

"Yeah, of course." Margaret shrugs, without missing a beat. "I was really busy. I had all these classes and then I also do personal training. It was a little bit easier because I don't have to do all of the sets with the client. I can print you off the schedule if you want to see it and I can give you info from different people who are in all these classes or you can access the details of all the people who participated in sessions right here."

"Yes. I'd like that," I say.

Sometimes people who are overly helpful have something to hide and I wonder whether in this case, this is exactly what Margaret is showing me. She logs into the Zoom sessions and shows me the recorded videos.

"Do you usually record them?"

"Yeah. Sometimes people can't make it and if they pay to be in my unlimited class program, I give them the link and they can watch the recording at their leisure."

She opens one file after another, showing me recordings of the classes that she taught, as well as the personal training sessions and all of the names of the clients who were there during the live classes. I ask her to send me all of these details to my work email address, so that the computer tech team can go through this in more detail, and she agrees. She uploads the files, and we both watch them go one at a time.

"What is going on with you and Robert now?" I ask, still holding her phone in my hand.

"We're done. When I heard about Karen's disappearance, I was just in shock, but we were done that afternoon when she showed up. I apologized to her and her friend profusely. I actually had no idea that they weren't separated or filing for divorce. I felt so bad for her. She was so upset, distraught, and I just knew that I'd caused all of that pain."

I scroll through her messages again and then click on the name at the top. It's labeled as Robert, but I want to see the actual number. I write it down and compare it to the one I have in my notebook. It's a match. He was texting on his phone.

"He didn't have another phone?" I ask.

"Yeah," she says, blushing and looks away. Her baby starts to fuss and she excuses herself and reappears a few minutes later with a little bundle in her arms.

"She's nine months old now," she says.

"How was Robert as a father?"

"Absent," she snaps. "I mean, he would come by and play, but when I asked him to move in, he said he wasn't ready. That should have been a sign to me. There have been so many signs," she says, shaking her head.

"Like what?" I challenge her.

"Like the fact that when we had a fight after Karen left and broke up for good, I asked him about the phone. I asked him what phone he used to talk to me? I wanted to know whether or not it was premeditated enough to go out there and buy one of those untraceable phones at Walmart. Like, was he that devious? Was he trying to deceive me that much?"

"What did he say?"

"He told me that he was using his regular phone. He said for a while Karen never cared, never looked, but then when she started to get a bit suspicious, he just made a different app and put our text messages in there. I don't know how that works exactly, but basically it was like a secret folder on his phone where he kept just our conversations."

I don't stay long after that. I give her my card and ask her to be in touch if she thinks of anything else. I have to. I also tell her to expect a call from me in the next few days, following up and possibly asking her to come in for an official interview. She looks at her schedule and says that she'll be able to move her classes around because she'd love to come in and talk to me more. She walks me out past her rose bushes, still holding the baby on her hip.

When I get back in my car, I look through my notes trying to make sense of Margaret Layne. When I came here, I thought I would meet a cagey woman who knew about her boyfriend being married and didn't particularly care about it, going so far as getting pregnant. After meeting her, I'm pretty certain that assessment is completely untrue. She gave me the sense of being honest and transparent, by showing me her phone, her laptop, and agreeing to come for an official interview.

It's something that has been done plenty by guilty people, but there's something else. She seemed to have real sympathy for Karen. I don't know whether she suspects Robert for sure. I got a pretty strong sense that she did, but I also feel like she was telling me the truth, that they broke up the afternoon that Karen and Elin caught them together.

Still, what if it's all an act? What if she's just a really good actress and she in fact did have something to do with Karen's disappearance? Robert could have told her what he was doing or maybe she threatened to leave him unless he divorced his wife and he wasn't ready to do that, but he was ready to kill her. These thoughts and about 100 other possibilities consume me like a flood of the unknown. Uncertain as to how to proceed just yet, I look at the time and head back out for some drinks with Mark.

24

I meet Mark at a little bistro right off of Fairfax called Glass. It has specialty cocktails along with some really nice hors d'oeuvres and no dinner. It's basically a bar, but with really good, tiny plates of food. When I get there a little bit after five, Mark is already waiting for me. He's sitting at the far end of the bar in a suit, tie, and shiny shoes glistening in the warm glow of the chandelier above him. As soon as I walk in, he waves me over and gives me a hug that's a little bit too long.

When our bodies touch, I can hear the beating of his heart through his dress shirt, a quality that he always seemed to have.

"How are you? So good to see you," he says, without taking his eyes off of me. "You look beautiful."

"Thanks." I nod quietly and force myself to look at the menu.

His hair is a little bit long in the front, but with that, giving him that smoldering expression. Beautiful. Bringing attention to his green eyes and his strong jaw.

"You're an attorney now?" I ask. "Really?"

"Yeah. Is that hard to believe?"

"Kind of. You weren't exactly particularly law abiding when we knew each other."

"Ha, what is that supposed to mean?"

"Drove too fast. Drank underage."

"Yeah, I guess so. Hey, listen," he says, "I don't even think you're allowed to be an attorney if you don't drink, but that's just between you and me."

I nod.

"How are you? What's new, Detective Carr?"

"Nothing. Just working cases. Mad hours. Same thing."

"Yeah. I know all about that. I felt law school was hard, but junior associate hours don't leave much time for a social life."

"What about this?" I ask when the bartender brings us two elderberry martinis with mint.

"Hey, this is happy hour/dinner. I hope they have food here." He laughs and tosses his hair confidently. "Then I'm back to the office."

"You are?"

"Yeah. Remember that client that I was meeting when we met?"

I flash back to how sweaty and ugly I felt that night and to say a silent prayer for the fact that my boobs look exquisite in this blouse and my butt looks perfect in this skirt.

"Well, I signed him and it's going to be a lot of work from now on."

"Can you tell me anything about it?" I ask.

He shakes his head no.

"Come on, please?" I plead.

"Okay. It would be a maybe if you weren't in law enforcement, but you work for the LAPD."

"Okay. How about not his name or anything specific? Just, what did he do?"

"What did he do allegedly?" he corrects me, and I roll my eyes. "Yeah. Those kinds of details never matter to cops, do they?" Mark says, taking a sip of his martini and I linger a little bit too long on his mouth touching the glass.

"You're really not going to tell me anything?" I ask.

"No. If I did, you'd probably be able to figure it out, so I'm going to keep this to myself for now until we go public."

"Okay. I give up," throwing my hands in the air demonstratively.

"Tell me about your case. What were you doing today?"

I inhale and exhale slowly, not really wanting to talk about this.

"Let's not," I say after a pause. "I've had a long day. I'm sure you did, too. Actually, I've had about a decade of long days and let's just be two normal people talking about something else, something fun. Okay?"

"Like what?"

"I don't know. Your turn," I say, finishing my drink a little too fast and asking the bartender for another.

The alcohol hits my head and I start to relax and the tension that I've been carrying around in my shoulders seems to vanish. My arms start to move freely around me rather than attach stiffly to my torso.

He stares at me, looks deep into my eyes, and suddenly my smile goes away, and the mood seems to change.

"You know, I'm surprised you wanted to meet here," I say quietly, "since you know The Grove is right over there."

"Yeah, I know, but I'm not sure if we're ready to walk down memory lane quite yet," he says, without looking away from me.

Memories start to flood in. I can't keep them out because my inhibitions have been lowered by the liquid courage coursing through my veins.

"You don't want to talk about the past?" I finally say, bringing my eyes back from the bar top to meet his one more time. "You don't want to talk about the present. What is it that you do want to talk about?"

He leans over to me and I get a whiff of his aftershave. It's exactly the same brand that he used in college.

Suddenly, I find myself back there, holding hands, spinning around in the rain after finals in the quad. He's so close to me.

I feel like he wouldn't even have to move an inch to kiss me, but instead he moves a little bit closer to my ear and whispers in it, "The future."

25

_____

I don't know exactly what he means by that, but our gazes remain locked for some time until the bartender asks if we want to refill our drinks. Once the trance is broken, I pull away. Uncertain as to what else to talk about, I bring up my case. This has always been kind of a default thing and something I wanted to avoid but talking about the truth with Mark seems impossible right now. I don't mention names or locations, but I do mention the missing wife, which piques his interest.

"Hope you're not interested in representing him already," I joke.

"No, not until you arrest him."

I laugh and he laughs along with me. For a moment, it feels like all of those years that separated us have disappeared or maybe were never even there in the first place. When the conversation reaches a natural ending point and it's time to start another, I pull away.

I have more work to do, as I know, does he. He walks me out and we stand next to each other right outside the front door, not exactly certain of how to say goodbye.

"I'd like to see you again," Mark says. I don't know if he means romantically or as a friend.

"Me, too." I nod. "This was nice, catching up, seeing what you were up to."

"Yeah, sorry that you couldn't stalk me on social media."

"Hey, listen. I'm sure that you stalked me. It's only fair, right?"

He laughs and then leans over and kisses me. When his lips collide with mine, I stand here for a moment lingering, but then pull away.

"No." I shake my head.

"I'm sorry, I thought that ..."

"No, I can't. I'm sort of seeing someone and, well, I don't know what that is, but I'm just ... I can't deal with this."

"Listen, I know that you work a lot of hours and so do I and that this seems complicated, but it was so nice being together again. Don't you feel like everyone you date, everyone you're with, you can never get back what you had back there in college and that maybe it was a mistake?"

"What?" I ask. "Breaking up?"

I look away from him. It would be a lie to say that that wasn't at least partly true. I've thought about him often, but it has also been years and I don't know if I'm the same person anymore. I don't know if I'm capable of being that happy. I don't tell him any of this. It would be too painful, and the conversation would take too much time that I don't have.

"Can I still see you again?" he asks. "Can we pretend that I never kissed you?"

I think about that for a moment.

"Yes," I say definitively.

He stands there with his hands to the sides, knowing full well after being turned down and unable to make another move. It's my turn. I reach over and give him a brief hug and an even briefer peck on the cheek.

"Call me," I whisper into his ear and walk away.

Later that evening after talking to my mom and Captain Talarico, but avoiding calling Luke just yet, I decide to stay in LA because there are no more updates about Violet or Natalie.

In the middle of the night, I get a call. A body has been found and there's a strong possibility that it belongs to my missing person, Karen Moore Kaslar. It's not necessary for me to drive up there right now at one a.m. They will be processing the scene and the body will be going to the morgue, but I can't help myself. I have to know if it's her. She fits the general description and I know that I won't be able to get any sleep tonight unless I confirm this for myself.

I get into my car and get on the freeway. After pulling my hair up into a loose ponytail and throwing some water on my face, I have a change of clothes and a makeup bag that I keep in the car in case any public is going to be there or any reporters. For now, I don't bother with any of that. The freeways are empty and I drive fast, but just barely over the speed limit.

GPS takes me deep into the hills and to a point where my phone loses reception. The roads are winding with little light, black trees, and deep forests lining each side. Finally, I get there. The scene has been set up not far from the trailhead. I flash my credentials at the deputy in the parking lot near the trailhead and he points me in the direction of the scene. I'm already wearing a pair of sneakers and I'm thankful for that because the body is about a mile and a half up. I walk by myself in the forest and the trail is eerie at night.

There's no light and I use my phone as a flashlight to illuminate my path. I trip a few times over a few loose stones. I get a cramp in my side and I regret not bringing a bottle of water. Finally, I see the tent out in the distance, with people mingling around, setting up, and processing the scene.

Detective Rodriguez, a family man in his mid-forties with five kids, the youngest of whom is already heading to college, meets with me to discuss the details.

"Glad you came," he says. "We just found her wallet. She's going to have to get identified by the next of kin, but it seems like it's her."

I walk over to the taped-up scene and see Karen's lifeless body lying on her stomach with her head twisted to the side. Her hair is matted down and the top of it is covered in blood.

"The rock used is right over there," Rodriguez says.

Somebody is photographing the palm-size piece of granite, also covered in blood.

I'll have to wait for the crime scene investigators, but it seems like a match to me. I take a few steps closer to look at her face. It's tilted toward me. It matches the woman from the pictures that I've seen. Straight nose, strong jaw.

"It's hard to tell whether she's been hit once or more than once," Rodriguez says. "This is likely the murder weapon."

"No bullet holes?"

"No. Well, not that I can see from here. They'll be processing the scene."

I nod. It's not unusual to find additional evidence and we have to wait until all of it comes in. I think to myself before drawing any conclusions, but there are already conclusions that can be drawn.

"How did she get here?" I ask.

"Most likely scenario," he says, pushing up his glasses to the top of his head, "she walked here.

The bastard who did this, walked her here of her own accord. Maybe they took a hike and then he did it here. There are no drag marks and unless he carried the body and dropped it off, it seems like a long way to go."

I nod thinking back to the trail that I had just walked. It's winding with lots of corners and I'm sure anyone would hesitate to carry a dead body all this way just to drop it along the side of the trail, without bothering to go deep into the forest.

"What about an ATV or any other alternative outdoor vehicle?"

"I didn't see that many marks or tracks leading up here. They're forbidden on the trails, but that doesn't mean that someone hadn't used one."

"Yeah, I didn't see any either," I say, thinking back to the trail that I had just walked and all of the details that I tried to notice on the way up here.

"Also didn't see any obvious droplets of blood, which might have happened if he had carried her body here."

"Any chance that she was wrapped up in anything? Like, I don't know, some sort of bag?"

"That seems unlikely, too. I was looking at her face and you can see right there that the blood is pretty much coagulated right where it formed. It seems unlikely that she was moved from this position at all, let alone, that she was wrapped up in anything and then transported."

"So, she walked here?" I say, biting my lower lip and looking around. There are flood lights illuminating the forest, casting long, jagged shadows in all directions. "Who found her?"

"Somebody called it in. We're still trying to track it, but they used a cell phone. It sounded like two girls, young twenty-somethings, had a strong Valley accent. Sounded a bit ditsy if you don't mind me saying."

"So, they never actually met you guys here?"

"No. They called about three hours ago, called 911, said that they were taking pictures and stumbled upon her, but they had to go and they couldn't stay and then they gave the information. We're going to track the phone, but it's going to take some time. We sent someone out here. A deputy was about to turn back thinking that it was just some sort of prank call when he stumbled upon her body right there."

"Wow."

"Yeah." Rodriguez nods. "I guess she's not a missing person anymore."

I take a few steps away from Rodriguez and take a closer look at the body. She's dressed in leggings and a sports bra, but no sweatshirt or a top layer. She looks like she has been here a long time.

Her face is blue, and the blood looks old. How long exactly? I'm not sure. The fact that she wasn't wearing a sweatshirt probably means that she went hiking during the day.

The state forest officially closes at sundown. It looks like some animals have already gnawed at her legs and arms. There is a lot of evidence of insect activity as well. I count back the days that she's been missing, though body evidence science is never that precise.

Once the body gets over a week old or probably even sooner than that, there're a lot of different experts with different opinions, but we are still in the early stages of finding out exactly the time of death.

Things like insect activity, location of the body, the heat, and the humidity all play a role in decomposition. A body that decomposes in the hot and humid sun in a place like Georgia has a different rate of decomposition than a body that would decompose in Alaska or California.

Here, the sun is strong and warm during the days, but the nights can drop as much as thirty to fifty degrees in temperature depending on the altitude. This is a desert after all, making the climate rather unique.

I lean down and get as close to her body as possible to look for details that might mean anything. She's wearing a gold locket, but I won't know what's inside until the medical examiner puts out her report.

She's wearing an Apple watch and I wonder if it might hold any clues as to how she got here or how far she'd walked. I point the watch out to Rodriguez, and he nods approvingly.

"Yeah, that's going to be the first thing we check out."

"Let me know as soon as you do. There may be apps on it that she used to track herself even if she didn't use the main walking app."

"Yes, I know I have one myself," he says. "Been trying to get those 10,000 steps in every day."

"How's that working?" I ask.

"Eh, some days better than others. All that time in the car isn't helping much. With the hike up here, I might get that 10K yet."

I smile. It may sound coarse and rude to talk like this, to make jokes, but this is our job.

We're not mocking the victim, not in the least.

We're just trying to make a terrible tragedy bearable for us to investigate it.

26

In the morning, after the Apple watch has processed, I get the result. Karen was recording her hike on a trail walking app and it showed that she started it in the parking lot on the day that her husband reported her missing, the eighteenth.

I don't bother going home after a few hours at the scene. So, I take a little cat nap in my car, get some coffee, and head back to the parking lot at the beginning of the trailhead.

Benjamin Lawrence, the computer tech who got up early to work on this as a personal favor to me, sends me the GPS coordinates of everything that the watch recorded. I start in the exact spot. I use my phone to line up my own GPS coordinates and start to follow her trail. Her walk up the trail precisely. It's morning now and I'm not limited to the flashlight or my phone for visibility.

The trail is winding with a steep incline. I follow the GPS coordinates as precisely as I can while also taking note of the trees, the vegetation, and the shrubs all around. I'm looking for blood droplets, anything that would indicate that she hadn't walked up there. I'm also looking for other things, maybe something that was dropped, or forgotten, or anything that could be of any significance whatsoever.

When I get almost to the top, to the location of the murder site, I head back down and do another loop. Nothing catches my eye until my shoelace unties and I kneel down to fix it.

I get a cramp in my back. I do a few stretches. This is the most exercise I've gotten in a while and my body is not ready for it.

I do a brief sun salutation and stretch from side to side.

That's when I see it.

The camera.

It's positioned toward the trail, going down toward the parking lot in the opposite direction that I'm walking. It's hidden. It's in the tree at about six feet up. There's a raven that sits on a branch just a little bit higher chirping loudly or rather obnoxiously.

I walk over to the camera for a closer look.

Am I really seeing what I'm seeing? Why would it be here?

Then I remember that this must be a trail camera, a webcam set up to monitor wildlife.

Sometimes they're used for tracking purposes, but they're also commonly set up on national forest and state park websites in order to get the public interested in going there. High school kids and younger kids will monitor the cameras for science classes. Occasionally there'll be a brown bear or a mountain lion who will do something interesting, funny, or cute and then it will go viral on YouTube.

I'm so excited by this discovery that I immediately start to run. It's a good quarter mile uphill and I'm completely out of breath when I get there. A ranger from the National Forest has already arrived and I ask him about the camera choking on my own breath.

"I just found it there, not too far away, by the big boulder," I say, my breathing is rapid and out of control. "There's a camera there. How long is that footage kept? Do you think that maybe she might be on it?"

"We actually stream it live and we do keep it for about two weeks," he says and then asks me for my name.

I realize that I haven't even introduced myself to him. We shake hands and he tells me to call him Michael and says that back in the office, he has access to all of the webcams that are set up around the forest.

"Okay. Can you show me where you have it? Can we go there right now?" I ask, finally catching my breath.

"Yes, of course." He nods.

Half an hour later, I park in front of the ranger station and Michael shows me inside. He's a young man in his early thirties with a wedding band and a crew cut.

He tells me that he's been working here for about five years and his wife isn't very happy with the hours or the salary. He has to decide whether or not he'll continue to work here and get divorced or go work for her father selling furniture and stay married.

I don't know how to advise him because I've never been in that situation. Personally, I kind of hope that he stays doing what he loves, despite all the obstacles.

At the ranger station, he takes me to a nondescript room with office furniture and a pinkish gray carpet that Michael apologizes for and says that they will finally be changing out in a month or two.

"It's not the best thing to have in a place where people walk around in muddy shoes," he says. "Bureaucracy. Other stations need other things."

He shows me to his desk, a metal clunky thing covered in papers and with drawers that make an obnoxious metal on metal sound. He opens his laptop and starts scrolling through the files on the eighteenth.

"Can you check that first? Maybe morning?" I ask. "How do you know which camera is which?"

"They're all numbered. That one is 4327," he says from memory. "Occasionally gets a few deer. Last year, I caught a mountain lion with a baby kitten. So, we had fun with that."

"Ever catch a murder suspect?"

"Nope. That'd be a new one for this." He smiles. "This is actually going to take a little bit. There're a bunch of files and I'm not sure what time they were. They get overwritten after a while."

"Okay. I understand," I say. "I'll wait."

"If you want, there's a vending machine out there if you're hungry."

"Sure. Can I get you anything?"

"Yeah, a pop," he says, and I immediately know that he's from the east coast.

27

I stay with Timothy for about an hour as he searches through the camera footage all without luck. I know that she went there, and we have the camera that was working. The question is what day did she actually go missing and was it later in the day than I thought? It's all very possible because I don't know exactly when she was there.

I tell him not to give up and to keep looking and that I'll send Benjamin, the computer tech, over here to get the footage. He says that he can't stay for long because he has a few department meetings to attend. So, he agrees to upload the footage from his computer for the LAPD computer professionals to look through.

I text and arrange everything and then get back into my car and sit here for a while trying to process what has happened. In the last few hours, there have been so many highs and lows. First, her body was found, and then she was identified as the woman, Karen Moore, that I've been looking for, but now I have no idea where to go from here.

Robert is the primary suspect, but so is his girlfriend, Margaret. She put on a good face but that doesn't mean that the two of them didn't lure her out somehow and get her to that trail.

While they continue to look through the footage, I drive down to Park La Brea. I need to go over some parts of the story with Elin again and tell her that we've found her friend's body. This is going to be difficult. Elin seems to be the only one who cares about Karen and it's going to break her heart.

I knock on her door and wait a few minutes for her to answer. Just as I'm about to give up, she opens the door with her finger over her mouth, telling me to be quiet.

"I just put the baby down," she whispers.

I nod and tiptoe into the apartment. It's probably not the best time to tell her the news but I don't have a choice.

"I have some bad news," I say, taking a deep breath. Elin's eyes grow wide and when I tell her about Karen's body, she begins to sob, burying her face in her hands.

It takes her a little bit to compose herself and I give her time before launching into my questioning.

"I just can't believe that this has happened."

"I was just wondering if you have any idea who she could have been hiking with."

"I don't know."

"There are some wildlife cameras set up, so the techs are going through the files now. Hopefully, we can get some answers."

We talk about it for a little bit and then I get a call. I excuse myself and walk out onto the patio so I don't wake up the baby.

"It's her," Captain Medvil says. "It's her."

A bird flies up and lands on the railing, distracting me.

"What?" I ask.

"Get out of there!"

Cold sweat runs down my back.

I reach for my gun, but then I feel the barrel of the gun at the nape of my neck.

"Give it to me," Elin says.

"Elin, what are you doing?" I say, as she reaches, as I freeze.

She reaches over and puts her hand on my weapon and pulls it out of the holster.

"You don't need this anymore," she says. "Be very quiet. My baby is sleeping."

That part is true. She keeps pressing the barrel of her gun to my neck and tells me to walk backward into the living room. She tells me to sit down and stands right across from me holding a 9mm pointed straight at me with one hand and my gun in her other.

The tears are gone.

The expression on her face is completely changed. She's like a chameleon.

There's a harshness to it now, a darkness. The pleasantness and the beauty of the friendly Elin that I had met before has vanished.

"What are you doing?" I ask.

She doesn't reply and Captain Medvil's words run through my mind.

"It's her," he says.

The video, he must have seen it. He must have seen her walking with Karen on that trail.

"Why are you doing this?" I ask, pretending that I have no knowledge about anything.

"Don't lie to me, Detective Carr," Elin says. "You've seen the footage on that wildlife cam. I know you have."

"I have no idea what you're talking about," I insist.

"You're not such a good liar after all."

She tucks my gun into the waist of her jeans and then holds hers straight out supporting the barrel with her other hand, just like we are taught in the police academy.

"What are you doing, Elin? Did you kill your friend?"

"She had it coming," she says, taking me by surprise. She was so good at playing this game.

Why is she suddenly coming forward? I clench my jaw.

"She was going to kill me. That's why. Someone should know, right? I did a pretty good job for my first time."

"What are you talking about?" I ask.

"Karen was no good," she says, shaking her head.

Suddenly I see a crack in her facade. The darkness seems to disappear only for a moment or perhaps it's just pity and sadness for herself.

"Tell me what happened. I can help you."

"You can't help me with anything. You think I killed her for nothing."

"Tell me what happened and what you did. I'm here to help you."

"You're a detective. You're here to find out what happened to the *victim*," she says, the coldness returns.

"Okay. Then what do you want to do?"

"I'm going to kill you," she says.

I swallow hard. I need to buy some time. I need to figure out a way to get out of here, but she's completely unpredictable.

One minute she's her best friend and another one she's this killer, which I never expected.

"You don't want to do that," I say slowly. "Whatever happened with Karen, you must have done it for a reason, right? There must have been a why. If you kill me to get away, that's not going to be good. Not for you, not for your baby."

"Don't bring my baby into this." She shakes her finger at me briefly letting go of the gun, but then quickly readjusts her grip.

I kick myself for missing my chance to grab it.

"That baby's the whole reason why I'm in this mess in the first place. He said he was going to leave her. He said that if we had a baby together, then we would be together."

"What?" My mouth drops open. Then it hits me. "The baby is Robert's?" I ask in a half whisper.

"Of course," she snaps. "Are you an idiot? Of course the baby is Robert's."

"How long were you seeing each other?"

"Long enough. Robert likes to have girlfriends on the side, and he likes to get them pregnant. That's what happened to Margaret right around the same time that he was seeing me. He started seeing *her*. How dare he cheat on me?" she snaps.

I blink a few times trying to make sense of everything that she's saying. Is she really mad at Robert for seeing another woman when he was already married and seeing her?

"He said that Karen didn't understand him. He said that I was the only one who did. He said he loved me. He said that he hadn't slept with Karen in months. Then I find out that he has a girlfriend in Reseda." She narrows her eyes.

"Why did you kill Karen? Why not Robert?" I ask.

"We were going to run away together. You happy to hear that? He was going to leave her. We were going to be together, but then I thought that if she found out about the affair, she would leave him, or he would finally leave her. I thought that would get the ball rolling."

"So, you found out about Margaret first?"

"I tracked him. Then I wanted Karen to find out. I wanted her to leave him so that he would be mine."

"What about Margaret?"

"That little skank? She never stood a chance."

I shake my head.

"You don't believe me?" she says, whispering because the baby in the other room starts moving around.

I just see it as she was dating a man who was already married and who got his mistress pregnant, he got her pregnant, and he got his wife pregnant all around the same time.

Why would she want to be with him in the first place? I want to ask, but I decide against it. My goal is to soothe her, relax her, and to get her to let her guard down.

"What about your husband?" I ask.

I shouldn't have asked that. I realized that that would just make her flare up even more. Her nostrils widen and she shakes her head.

"I don't need you judging me, or my actions. Okay? You're a dead woman already."

I think she wants me to beg for my life, but I'm not going to. I also think that she wants to tell me what happened.

Sometimes when people do something extraordinary, I don't mean great, but so huge and monumental like this, they want people to know about it.

"My husband is a fool," Elin says. "Things have been off with us for a long time. It didn't help that I started seeing Robert. Robert and I had all these plans that we were both going to leave our spouses and be together, but time just kept slipping by and he wouldn't do anything. I got pregnant. I was going to tell my husband and he was going to tell Karen, and that would be the end of it."

"So, what happened?" I ask, taking a deep breath.

"I found out that he was cheating on me."

I blink.

She notices it and explains, "With Margaret."

"How did you find out?"

"Karen was stupid. Karen believed everything he said. She thought that they had this happy marriage, but I was the one who had to tell her about checking his text messages. I was the one who had to tell her about putting a GPS on his car. I did that first. That's how I found out about Margaret. That's how I found out about his other baby and that he had no plans of leaving Karen."

"I still don't understand," I whisper. "Why did you take her out there? Why did you take her hiking? Why did you do that to Karen?"

"You don't know anything, do you?" Elin snaps.

She takes two steps away from me and then forward again. She's pacing. She's trying to figure out how much she wants to tell me.

"Karen got pregnant. She got pregnant and that meant that Robert was never going to leave her.

He told me he wouldn't. He told me he was already married and if Karen got pregnant, that would be it. He'd stop fooling around with me."

"What about the children?"

"I don't care about her child," she hisses.

"Okay. What about yours?"

"He said that Karen could never find out. He said he wanted her to be a secret. It's like he didn't care that we had all these plans. He didn't care that our baby existed. He was going to start a new life with his wife. That was just unacceptable." She looks away for a moment.

A tear builds up in her eye and that's when I lunge at her. I topple her over and we fall onto the coffee table, which snaps under us.

She kicks me between my legs, and I throw her hands over her head trying to knock the firearm out of her grip. It takes a few tries before it actually works, but not before she shoots a bullet through the window.

I punch her in the stomach and then climb over her to grab the gun but she pulls me down and wraps her long fingers around my neck and starts to squeeze.

She squeezes hard.

I try to punch her in her sides, but with my airway closing, I start to feel weaker and weaker.

She climbs on top of me, the weight of her body pressing me into the floor. She lets go briefly and I gasp for air and reach for her to stop her from getting the gun.

She presses on my windpipe with the weight of her body. I don't have much time.

With all of the strength that I have left, I start to feel around with both hands for something sharp or heavy or both to get her off of me.

She pulls away from me and I get another big gasp of air. That's when I see the gun in her hand again, the barrel right in front of my face.

"Goodbye, Detective Carr," she says.

At the last moment, my fingers curl around something sharp and I stab her in the neck with it.

Blood sprays out covering both of us. She cries out in pain and I grab the gun, moving it out of the way just in time for a bullet to hit the floorboard right next to my ear.

The sound deafens me.

I pull the sharp object out of her neck and stab her again and again, blood gushing out, but I don't stop until she's dead.

After I push her limp body off of me, I get up.

I sit up and stare at the carnage with tears running down my cheeks.

My breaths are still haphazard and sporadic, but at least I'm breathing.

"I'm okay," I say out loud just to make sure that I can hear.

28

A fter police and the ambulance arrive, they clean me up and take my statement. I don't have any injuries that require me to go to the hospital, but I do have a pounding headache.

Armed with a few Advil, I head back to the precinct to give my account and get a fresh change of clothes. Captain Medvil meets me up front and gives me a hug.

"I'm glad you're okay, kiddo," he says.

I smile. It's the first time he's ever called me that. I appreciate it.

We go to the conference room, the unofficial interrogation room used for police officers. I pull out the recorder and place it on the table.

"What's this?" Captain Medvil asks.

"I had it in my pocket when I went out on the patio to talk to you. I started it as soon as she sat me down on the couch. I hope it got at least part of what happened."

We rewind the tape and plug it into the computer. Our whole conversation comes on loud and clear, except for a few places where the recorder rubs against the inside of my pocket.

Everyone listens, but I have to excuse myself because I can't bear to relive it quite yet, if ever.

A little bit later, a deputy calls me back in.

"You had to do what you did," Captain Medvil says. "You know that, right?"

"Yeah. Just would have been nice if it went to trial and everything came out in the open."

"Well, we're still going to investigate. We're going to get to the bottom of this, but from that conversation and from what we found on the tape, I don't think that Robert or Margaret were involved," the captain says.

I nod.

"We'll do more interviews, but right now you need to go home and get some rest."

After I get home, I sleep for what feels like days, but it's really just a very long twenty-four hours. The findings from the medical examiner confirm that Karen was indeed pregnant at the time of her death.

We find a lot of evidence on Robert's laptop that corroborates the relationship that he had with Elin going back years.

In another interview, not conducted by me, he confirms that he did indeed have a relationship with Elin. At one point, they'd planned on leaving their spouses, but he wanted to try to make it work with Karen, despite the fact that he had two children with two other women.

The reason it seems why he was so cagey with me in all of the interviews is that he didn't want anyone to find out about those children, least of all Karen.

Elin had lured her out on that walk and she may have told her everything, or perhaps she pretended that she was her friend until the end. We will never know. I didn't get a chance to ask, and there are just certain things that people take to their graves.

When I wake up, I see that I have a number of missed calls from Luke along with a number of messages telling me that someone had called him about what had happened and that he wants to know how I'm feeling.

His voice is concerned, sweet, and loving. I want to talk to him more than anything. The fifth time he calls that evening, I answer.

He immediately gets onto FaceTime, even though at first, I don't want to get on. I look tired and worn out, but he tells me that I look beautiful, which given how I exhausted I am, is an exaggeration if not a complete lie.

"I wish I were there," Luke says. "I should have helped you."

"Helped me with what? This is my case."

"I know. I just keep blaming myself."

"There's no reason for that. You're investigating my sister's case. I just should have brought backup, but I'm glad that it all worked out."

"So, you killed her with a pencil, huh?" he asks, rubbing his fingers across his lower jaw.

He looks so sexy and beautiful. I can't help but lick my lips as I imagine his arms around me.

"Yeah, that's what they told me. All I knew was that it was sharp and pointy, and that was the only thing I found."

"That's some spy crap right there," he laughs, "disarming an enemy with a pencil."

I laugh and so does he.

Making light of the dark is the only way to get through this. We talk some more, and we laugh.

For a little while, it feels like we're normal people, a normal couple even, catching up on the day.

Then my thoughts return to Violet. When I ask about her, his face drops.

"What?" I ask. "Did you find something? Did you find *her*?"

He shakes his head no but doesn't say a word.

"Tell me," I insist. "What is it?"

"We found the clothes that she was wearing that night," he says quietly, "about a mile away from the observatory."

"What do you mean?"

"We found her puffy forest green jacket, jeans and a beanie as well as her Uggs. Your mom confirmed that the clothes are hers and Nancy,

Kaylee's mom, confirmed that she dropped her off wearing those clothes."

"I don't understand." I gasp.

"We found every single thing that she was wearing, Kaitlyn," Luke says. "Down to the socks and the necklace."

"Why would she change her clothes?" I ask, not really expecting an answer.

"There's something else," he continues after a long pause. I hold my breath.

"All the clothes were found neatly folded in a plastic bag tucked under a fallen tree."

"What does that mean?" I shake my head.

"I have no idea," he says, "but we're going to find out."

THANK YOU FOR READING! I hope you loved Detective Kaitlyn Carr's investigation. The next book in the Kaitlyn Carr series is **GIRL FOUND**....

A college student is found dead in the apartment of a US Marine who has disappeared.

Where is he? Did he kill her and run? And if so, why? **Detective Kaitlyn Carr will stop at nothing to find out what happened.**

Back home, Violet's disappearance is becoming a cold case to everyone but Kaitlyn. Every lead has been a dead end, but she can't give up now…

One-Click GIRL FOUND now!

Can't get enough of Kaitlyn Carr? Make sure to grab **GIRL HIDDEN (a novella) for FREE!**

A family is found dead in their home. The only survivor is the teenage daughter who managed to escape the burning house.

Who killed them? And why? **Detective Kaitlyn Carr has to bring their killer to justice.**

A year before her disappearance, Violet, Kaitlyn's sister, comes to stay with her after a bad fight with their mom. She can't stand living at home as much as Kaitlyn once did and wants to move in with her.

What happens when the dysfunction of her own family threatens to blow up her face and let the killer off for good?

GRAB GIRL HIDDEN for FREE now!

IF YOU ENJOYED THIS BOOK, please take a moment to write a short review on your favorite book site and maybe recommend it to a friend or two.

You can also join my Facebook group, Kate Gable's Reader Club, for exclusive giveaways and sneak peeks of future books.

WANT TO BE THE FIRST TO KNOW ABOUT MY UPCOMING SALES, NEW RELEASES AND EXCLUSIVE GIVEAWAYS?

Sign up for my newsletter:
https://www.subscribepage.com/kategableviplist

Join my Facebook Group:
https://www.facebook.com/
groups/833851020557518

Bonus Points: Follow me on BookBub and Goodreads!

https://www.goodreads.com/author/show/
21534224.Kate_Gable

ABOUT KATE GABLE

Kate Gable loves a good mystery that is full of suspense. She grew up devouring psychological thrillers and crime novels as well as movies, tv shows and true crime.

Her favorite stories are the ones that are centered on families with lots of secrets and lies as well as many twists and turns. Her novels have elements of psychological suspense, thriller, mystery and romance.

Kate Gable lives in Southern California with her husband, son, a dog and a cat. She has spent more than twenty years in this area and finds inspiration from its cities, canyons, deserts, and small mountain towns.

Write her here:

Kate@kategable.com

Check out her books here:

www.kategable.com

Sign up for my newsletter:
https://www.subscribepage.com/kategableviplist

Join my Facebook Group:
https://www.facebook.com/
groups/833851020557518

Bonus Points: Follow me on BookBub and
Goodreads!

bookbub.com/authors/kate-gable

https://www.goodreads.com/author/show/
21534224.Kate_Gable

amazon.com/Kate-Gable/e/B095XFCLL7

facebook.com/kategablebooks

bookbub.com/authors/kate-gable

instagram.com/kategablebooks

ALSO BY KATE GABLE

All books are available at ALL major retailers! If you can't find it, please email me at **kate@kategable.com**

Girl Missing (Book 1)

Girl Lost (Book 2)

Girl Found (Book 3)

Girl Hidden (FREE Novella)